Diego Champagne, Sergeant in Arms for the Louisiana Banni motorcycle gang, has grown up tough — half French, half Creole, and all male. Diego loves men but keeps his sex life on the down-low . . . until he meets Colby Young.

Colby carries his own baggage. He has his own reasons for not believing in love — reasons he doesn't share — and he sure as the devil doesn't like it when he's forced to accept help from anyone.

When Diego intervenes in a bar brawl during a motorbike rally and saves Colby and his best friend, Spider McGraw, leader of the rival gang Death Proof, it begins to look as if Colby and Diego are going to be joined at the hip. Somebody puts a hit out on Colby, and Spider's up to his neck in mayhem. When the Banni offer their protection to advance their own game, Colby begins to wonder: is love like artificial moonlight, seductive yet false? Or is it powerful and true, something for which he might risk everything . . . maybe even his life?

Content Advisory: This is a re-edited, re-release title.

Artificial Moonlight
Copyright © 2019 A.J. Llewellyn and D.J. Manly
ISBN: 978-1-4874-2514-2
Cover art by Martine Jardin

Published by eXtasy Books Inc or
Devine Destinies, an imprint of eXtasy Books Inc

Look for us online at:
www.eXtasybooks.com or www.devinedestinies.com

Artificial Moonlight
Rough Riders Book 1

By

A.J. Llewellyn and D.J. Manly

DEDICATION

To the men and women who love motorbikes, and those of us who love them.

"It takes more love to share the saddle than it does to share the bed."
— Author Unknown

"All our dreams are made of chrome."
— Tom Waits

CHAPTER ONE

Diego

A sign announcing that Austin was coming up in fifty miles made me want to cry out with jubilation. We were headed to the Travis County Exposition Center on the east edge of Austin, Texas, for their mega annual bike rally. It was only a seven to eight-hour drive from Baton Rouge to Austin, but with the way I was feeling, it felt like I was on the road trip that would never end. My bruised ribs weren't completely healed, and riding for this length of time had been murder.

We'd made one stop in some place called Oak Island, and I'd almost screamed when I got off my Harley. Then Chase wanted to get going ten minutes later. I suspected he had some party planned later with a couple of large-breasted clones. Most likely blondes.

Just before we left, some big bastards in an underground bar down in the bayou had jumped Chase for making a pass at their women. As sergeant in arms, I had no choice but to get into it. I was pissed at Chase—and still am, actually. It would be a really good thing if he could keep it in his pants once in a while. He was forever getting me into shit, and especially good at taking me completely unaware when we were supposed to be sticking to business. Not to mention that I'd just healed from the injuries I'd sustained at the extreme fight competition, an underground contest in Louisiana where the last man standing always won tons of money, along with the people who bet on him. Chase and the guys always cleaned up at these things.

I almost told him to fuck the bike rally this year, but then that wouldn't have flown with the club, so here I was in pain, as usual, riding mile after mile in the scorching sun.

Chase gave the signal to pull over now, so we all followed suit. The vice president and I pulled up on either side of Chase.

The vice president's nickname was Nuts, earned because . . . well, frankly, the guy was fucking crazy, and he was constantly eating nuts of every variety.

"Champagne." Chase looked at me. "You sure the hang arounds got our camping spots staked out?"

Chase pronounced my family name like the bubbly stuff you drank at New Year's, but my name was French, and it was pronounced ChamPang. I tried to correct him a few times. He didn't get it.

"I don't want any trouble with the law," Chase added, pulling off his helmet to reveal his long, ginger-colored braid and matching beard.

I shrugged. "I assume they arranged everything. They left yesterday."

Hang arounds were wannabe gang members, one step behind the prospects. We had at least ten wannabes, which translated into a lot of grown men doing whatever we need-ed done, for nothing. There was only one prospect. That might have been a clue to anyone wanting to join the club. Chase wasn't easily given to making people full-fledged members.

The prospect's name was Arnold. He followed us every-where and was Chase's devoted slave. Chase was calling him on the cell now.

Nuts, almost three hundred pounds with a scar all the way down one side of his chubby face, was shoving cashews into his mouth as he watched him. After Chase hung up, Nuts mumbled something neither of us could understand.

Chase punched Nuts in the arm and knocked the cashews out of his hand.

"Hey," he protested, pointing to the nuts scattered on the road. "Those are the last of what I got, brother."

"Smarten up. Stop eating so much. Get on your phone, idiot, and call up one of those stupid bastards. Make sure we know where to go this year."

We'd brought camping gear. Didn't cost anything to camp but you had to pay to park the hog. Chase wanted to make sure we had our own space. Last year we'd gotten into all kinds of trouble with other outlaw clubs wanting to fuck with us over territory on the campground, and the Texas Troopers, of course, got into it.

Banni de Louisiane, translated loosely as "banished from Louisiane," was well known in Texas. We had a reputation for being badasses. But we never messed with ordinary folk. Our appearance at these things, however, somehow sparked the testosterone of every pecker wearing a motorcycle patch this side of the Mississippi.

It was a piss-off when all we really wanted to do was enjoy the rally. We never came here to do business. We were on vacation. I suggested to Chase that we remove our colors for the rally, but I might as well have suggested we piss on them.

Arnold drove up in the van that held all our gear. He stuck his head out the window. "Hey, boss, what's up?" He was a skinny kid with glasses. He looked as if he should be in a science lab rather than hanging out with bikers. I couldn't believe he'd been waiting over five years for membership.

"Is our place staked out?"

"Yes, Chase. I heard from Marcel, and he said everything's cool, man."

"Good. Let's move then."

Arnold reached out the window and handed Nuts a small bag.

Nuts looked inside and grinned. "Cashews. Hey, thanks, man."

"Picked 'em up when we made the stop. Figured you'd be out."

Chase rolled his eyes.

I laughed.

Arnold turned and drove back down to the end.

We were on the road again, and traffic got heavier as we drew closer. We were forced to slow down. I wanted off this damn bike. I was finding it hard to breathe, actually, but I'd tough it out like I always did, looking forward to at least four days in one place, even if it was sleeping in a tent.

The sun was dipping lower in the sky, and I could feel the cool air on my face. It felt better, but I hoped it didn't rain during the night. I didn't relish floating on the roof of a tent come morning. I wasn't a camper.

We were approaching Austin now, riding in formation. Some car had cut in front of me, and we were moving at a crawl. There was traffic all around, and I took off my helmet for a minute. As I did, I heard someone whistle. I looked around, thinking I was hearing things. It was a wolf whistle, directed at me as if I were a chick or something.

I turned my head to the sound and saw two young guys in a sports car. Wow, that took balls, whistling at me. Guess they didn't notice I was wearing a biker's jacket, or they didn't know what it was. I quickly looked away—best to pretend I didn't hear them.

I was shocked that they'd do that because aside from the obvious fact that I belonged to an outlaw biker gang, I was pretty damn intimidating to look at. I was over six-foot-six of pure muscle, with shoulders like a linebacker. In fact, I had been a linebacker. Would have made the pros, too, but that was a long, sad story. One I didn't revisit often. Sure I had long, dark hair, and chicks said I was good-looking, but damn, I couldn't remember a guy being gutsy enough to whistle at me before.

Oh well. If they were cute, I didn't want to know. My entire existence belonged to the Banni now, and I didn't have time for much else, except keeping Chase out of trouble and protecting his sorry ass. Not saying it had always been like that. I'd once had a life, and I'd had plenty of sex with guys, but that kind of sex happened mostly in my head now. That kind of thing wouldn't be tolerated in the club. Any fucking I managed to do was fast and in the shadows. I had access to women whenever I wanted, but I rarely had the appetite for them, except out of desperation.

The lane I was in was standing still, and the sports car moved right up beside me. I kept my gaze straight ahead, tightening my hands on the handlebars.

Nuts was way out ahead with Chase. They'd stopped for a traffic light. A quick glance in my mirror told me there were several cars between me and the rest of the club.

"Hey, baby," the driver called out, sticking his head out a little. "You are so hot. What's your name, beautiful?"

I glanced at him now in disbelief. Yeah, he was cute. Too damn cute.

I smirked and then gave him the finger.

He stabbed at his chest with his fist, as if I'd shot him. The other guy laughed.

"Oh come on," the guy pleaded. "Don't do this to me, baby. I want to worship at your feet. I want you to ride me like you ride that bike. Tell me your name, please?" he called out. "Please tell me your name, or I might just die."

I tried not to smile, but he was pleading and groaning like

an idiot, putting on quite the show. It was pretty funny.

"You here for the rally, sweet man? I'm riding in the parade. I have a nice bike. I'll let you ride . . . it . . . I'll let you ride me . . . I know you have a fine ass too . . . and man, you are a big boy."

I didn't look directly at him, but I could see him in my mirror. I managed to go forward a little.

The car beside me moved up so fast, it almost hit the bumper of the one ahead. It stopped just in time. I wanted to laugh as the driver hollered out. "Shit! Look, darlin'. You're making me crazy. I almost had an accident. At least tell me your name, gorgeous? Tell me that I have a chance of feasting my eyes on you again, the most beautiful man I've ever seen . . . running into you on the street even, drooling over you from a distance? Anything? Tell me, how big is your cock? I know it could do the job, hit the spot. I'm dying here. Tell me your name, baby."

I heard his passenger say, "Colby, stop it!" Then they both started laughing like idiots.

"I'm in love!" the driver hollered.

I put my helmet back on and shook my head in despair. I prayed the traffic would move so I could push ahead and get away from this guy in his fancy Corvette. I should have gotten off my bike and kicked his ass for what he was saying to me, but for some reason, I didn't.

There was a break in traffic suddenly, and I sped ahead. I could see the car in the other lane keeping pace. Damn it. At the first chance, I squeezed in between two cars and almost got hit as the car behind me laid on his horn. I sped off down a side street and pulled over on the corner. I was breathing hard as I took off the helmet. I half expected to see that car coming down the street, but no, he couldn't have followed me. Crazy bastard!

The whole incident had really thrown me. Worse, it had

turned me on. A guy who wasn't afraid to talk to me like that had balls, even if he was really asking for trouble. And I kinda liked it.

If we met up again, I could wipe the floor with him and leave him bleeding and begging for death. Or I could fuck his tight, little ass all night long. Who would know . . . if he was willing? That guy wanted it, and he wanted it from me. Just maybe—if I saw him again and I could get him off by himself—I'd give it to him. I'd give him a rough ride. He wouldn't sit down for a month, and he'd never forget it either.

I smiled at that thought, then put on my helmet and drove back toward the main road. I couldn't wait to be at the campgrounds. I needed a shower and something to drink. I was also hungry, but I could wait on that.

When I arrived, I paid the parking fee, secured my bike, and went to locate the others. Chase and Nuts had found beer and were sitting under a tree right at the end of the field.

Chase looked up at me when I approached. "You seen the others?"

"They got cut off. They'll be along. A lot of traffic. Where are the hang arounds?"

Nuts handed me a cold beer. "They've gone to do the registering and shit."

I nodded my thanks and popped the cap. I leaned against the tree and drank down half of it. It felt good to move around. "Any food around here?"

"Want me to go get you some burgers, Diego?" One of the hang arounds asked. They were like trained puppies.

"I'll get something later," I said.

"How's the ribs?" Chase cocked an eyebrow at me.

"Okay, now that I'm not riding. No thanks to you, asshole," I looked at him.

7

"You need to be in shape for the fight in a few months."

"Yeah," I said. "No worries."

He stood. "Well, one of you guys come with me, the other can wait here and supervise the setting up. I got a meeting."

"I'll stay," I said. "I'm beat. I want a shower, and I want to sleep. Any place for a shower around here?"

"I think you gotta pay." Nuts hooked a thumb. "Careful. Don't get accosted by some pervert." He chuckled and drained his beer can.

I narrowed my eyes. "Fuck you." I looked at Chase. "I thought we weren't doing business this time."

"It's a brief meeting, nothing I can't handle. Just a little connection with a Texas gang I want to secure."

I nodded.

Arnold was coming with the van now. He stopped to speak with Chase and Nuts, drove up to where I was standing, and parked.

"Perfect," I said, going around back. I wanted my stuff.

I opened the door. Dave and Camden, two of the other members, jumped on me and knocked me to the ground, hollering like fiends. I swore and pushed them away.

"Boo," Dave said, poking out his hand.

I took it, and he pulled me to my feet. We laughed.

"Where are the others?" I asked.

"They're going with Chase and Nuts," Camden said. "That Marcel is coming with more of his pals. They'll set shit up."

I climbed in the back of the van and found my bag. I really wanted a shower. "Arnie, where are the showers?" I asked him when I was back on the ground.

"Want me to take you?" he asked as he began to pull out the tents.

"No, you got your hands full. Just point the way."

"You gotta walk all the way down there." He pointed. "I

think you got to pay something, or it might be included in the price. Don't know."

I shrugged. "Okay." I slung my duffle bag over my shoulder and walked down the path. On either side of me, people were settling in with their trailers and tents. Either people nodded at me or turned away when they saw me. That was pretty typical. I struck fear in people's hearts. It was the vest with the shrunken head hanging on a stick and the big, bold letters declaring me a member of the Banni de Louisiane. The patches on the front indicated that I was sergeant in arms. To people in the know, it meant that my job was to kick ass. And my size confirmed I'd have no trouble doing that.

I found the showers. I checked my watch and saw that it was eight o'clock, which explained the throng of kids in a variety of superhero pajamas all brushing their teeth over this trough-like thing with continual water running.

Some of the kids ran into me and squealed. I laughed as they ran off to their respective tents. I walked into the shower room on the men's side. They were free to use. There were ten independent showers stalls with a separate space to leave your stuff while you showered.

I took off my watch, my boots, and my clothes, and laid them carefully on the allotted shelf. I took special care with the vest. I found shampoo and soap in my kit, took a towel out of my bag, then got under the spray. The water wasn't too hot, but it didn't matter. I shampooed my hair, rubbed a hand over my rough jaw, and decided a shave could wait. I'd find a barber somewhere in the next day or two. I checked my ribs and noticed the bruising was almost gone.

I dried off and put on some clean clothes—jeans, my boots, and pulled a navy-blue T-shirt over my head. I rubbed the excess water out of my hair and brushed it out. I felt like a new man.

I picked up my vest and carried it outside, along with my bag. I'd taken two steps when I heard, "Well, hello, handsome. I guess it must be fate."

I couldn't believe my eyes when I saw him standing there. "The car guy? Shit. You gotta be kidding me!"

He laughed and came closer. Now that I had a good look at him, oh baby, did I like what I saw. His hair was thick and dark brown, and he had blue eyes — beautiful blue eyes — and a generous mouth. He was about six feet tall, nice and slim, with some intriguing tone. He was wearing a red muscle shirt and a pair of jean shorts. Those shorts were tight in all the right places.

"Is that what you call me?" He chuckled. "How cute. The car guy. Name's Colby, actually, but you can just call me 'baby.'"

I shook my head. "Do you know who I am?"

His gaze moved to the vest in my hand. "From the looks of it, you're some big shot with the Banni."

"You could get killed talking to me like that."

"I could die looking into your eyes; that's for sure."

"Well . . ." I cleared my throat, looking around. "That could be arranged."

"The dying or the looking into your eyes part?"

"Both," I told him.

"Woohoo, a macho man, threatening to kill me now. I would wager," He moved closer and placed a hand on my chest. "You'd have a hell of a lot more fun fucking me than killing me."

"Who are you?" I shook my head in wonder and pushed his hand away.

"Told you, my name is — "

"No, no, I mean . . . damn it, boy."

He smiled. "You like my style?"

"If you like the suicidal type, I guess."

10

He laughed. "You have a sense of humor."

"What are you doing here? Surely you're not sleeping here in this place."

"Why? 'Cause I have a fancy car?"

"Yeah, because you have a fancy car," I mocked.

He laughed again. "If you think I'm a little rich boy, you'd be right. At least, my daddy is."

"Where are you from?"

"The same place you're from, sweetheart. Good, old Louisiana. And you're Cajun."

"How would you know that?"

"I just do. You look it. And although you speak very good English, you sound Cajun. There's a lovely little twang in your voice. You might have a good mix of Creole too... Spanish and ... French, even a little café au lait?"

He was right on. My mother was Creole.

"It's incredibly intoxicating and sexy. In fact, you radiate sex. How bloody tall are you anyway?"

I didn't answer. "You're a little crazy, aren't you?"

"Maybe." He cocked his head. "But I'm the type of guy who knows what he wants when he sees it." He licked his lips, reached over, and grabbed a strand of my hair.

I knocked his hand away.

"You're still wet. I could've come in there and licked you dry."

"Really? How helpful of you."

"I want you. In fact, I want to wrap myself in that long hair of yours. I don't care if you're a biker, a dancer, or you work for the French Foreign Legion. I want what's in those pants. And you know what?" He moved up beside me and seemed to inhale me. "You want me, too. In fact, right now you're thinking about how you'd like to drag me into that shower you just got out of and fuck the hell out of me. You want to pump me until I beg for mercy, and then fuck me all over again."

I was breathless. Damn it. He could read my mind, and believe me, it was rated triple X. "Where are you staying?" I asked him, glancing around.

"I have a hotel room, all to myself." He met my gaze. The meaning was clear. "If you have balls like I think those colors you wear imply, you'll come by later and check out what I have to offer." He pulled a piece of paper and a pen out of his pocket, scribbled something, then pressed the piece of paper in my hand. "Address and room. It's a suite, really. It's got a hot tub."

I cleared my throat. "Don't hold your breath."

"I have some friends waiting for me. I promised to join them for a bonfire. I'll be at the hotel around midnight. I'll wait up." He met my gaze again. "Unless you're scared."

"Scared?" I raised my eyebrow. "Scared of what? You?"

He smiled. "You did almost get yourself killed, racing away from me earlier."

I scowled.

He laughed again. "Gotcha, beautiful."

"You like to play dangerous games, don't you?"

"Yes," he said. "I do. And you are the most dangerous and delicious game I've ever played. Jesus, you make my head spin."

"You could end up hurting."

"I'll take my chances. That's part of the thrill, isn't it? Now, if you were as willing to push the envelope as I am, you'd kiss me right now."

I took a step. I almost grabbed him and pulled him into the bushes, but then I saw Marcel heading toward me. "Get lost," I told him, and I crumpled up the paper and pushed it into my pocket.

"On one condition," he said. "Tell me your name."

"Diego," I grunted. "Now go."

He walked off in the other direction just as Marcel came up and took my bag. "How was the shower?"

"Fine," I said. I'd broken out in a damn sweat.

"We're set up. You hanging around or going somewhere?"

I took a breath. I glanced at the bonfire a few feet away. I could see the guy sitting there, talking and laughing with his friends. I knew his gaze was on me as I walked by with Marcel. I didn't look in his direction. "I'm going to get some sleep," I told him. "I'm beat."

My tent was ready when I got back. I said a few words to the guys, then crawled into the sleeping bag inside my tent. I knew I wasn't going to be able to sleep, not only because the other guys were talking loudly, but also because I couldn't stop thinking about that insane Colby guy. He was crazy gorgeous, and he wanted me, and that was wildly exciting. I knew I could get up and leave at any time, find my way to his hotel. I had only to put my jeans back on, reach in, and pull out the crumpled piece of paper I'd shoved into my pocket. I'd ride downtown, have a drink at one of the bars, and then if I still felt like it, I could drop by his room. Maybe I'd just fuck him and leave. What was the harm in that? He'd invited me, hadn't he? He was some kind of crazy.

What the hell.

CHAPTER TWO

I must have lain there about an hour before I made up my mind. I pulled on my jeans, slipped the navy T-shirt back on, then pulled on some socks and stepped into my boots. I took my leather jacket out of my bag, the one without the colors. I didn't want any hassle in the bars, and wearing the patch was an invitation to some yahoo wanting to take on a Banni.

When I came out of the tent, my helmet dangling off my fingers, a few of the guys were sitting around the fire. Marcel called out to me. "Going for some Austin pussy?"

"Something like that," I muttered. I didn't say that I was going after something a whole lot better than that, and it was homegrown.

I walked through the campgrounds toward the parking lot. I noticed that some people were dousing the fire, getting ready for bed. Others were still singing and drinking and dancing around.

I glanced over to the place where Colby had been sitting a while back. It was dark. He'd left already.

I dug my hand into the pocket of my jeans, pulled out the keys to my bike, and the crumpled paper along with it. He was at a five-star hotel in a suite—number four. He'd been slumming here at the campground for sure. That shit cost money.

He'd made a note.

Go to the front desk and ask for Colby Young.

I pushed the paper back into my pocket and walked over to where my bike was parked. I shrugged into my jacket and put on my helmet. I roared my Harley to life and headed in the direction of downtown. I followed the lights. In Austin, it was artificial moonlight that lit the city at night. Quite pretty. And because it didn't have big skyscrapers like in LA or New York, you actually got a good view of the skyline.

I'd been almost everywhere straddling this bike, from Georgia to Florida and up to Canada, where the Rockies of BC took your breath away. This bike was my good friend.

I loved this time of night—the warm breeze in my face, the freedom to go anywhere, do anything. It's the way I'd felt on the field with a football in my hand. All I'd been able to see was the wide-open space and that magic line where the touchdown happened.

Sixth Street was where all the clubs were in Austin. Once I got downtown, I remembered being on the street last year at this time, all the motorbikes lining both sides, the music, and dancing. As I continued on, I noticed it was packed with people, a lot of biker folk dressed in leather with big, rather hideous tattoos. I had a tattoo on my back of the Banni, but other than that, I wasn't that fond of tattoos. The one on my back had hurt like hell going on.

I found a place to park the bike and shoved my jacket into the saddlebag on the back. It was too damn hot to wear it.

I figured I looked very ordinary in my jeans and T-shirt as I negotiated my way through the groups of people. Some said hello to me as I walked. I got a few propositions from hookers, which I ignored.

I kept walking. I could see the hotel in the distance. I found a place on one of the side streets. I stood across from the building, watching the doorman open and close doors for the guests. I wasn't ready to go in yet. I guess I needed a drink or two.

I turned around and went back to Sixth Street. I walked into the first lively bar I came to. People were dancing and having a good time. Some country rock band was really swinging up on the stage. I stood at the bar and ordered a beer, glancing around at all the people.

A girl made eye contact with me, and I looked away. If Colby hadn't been leading me on, I had my fuck for the night. And it had been a long time coming. The last guy I'd had was three months ago. And the bugger gave out on me about a half hour into it.

The band started playing a slow song, and the girl came over and asked me to dance. I wished I'd worn my colors. That would have scared her off. She was a sweet thing. I didn't want to hurt her feelings. I told her I had an injury and I couldn't dance.

She hung around a while, staring at me. I began to feel uncomfortable. I checked my watch. It was after midnight. I excused myself and left the bar. If things were different in my life, I wouldn't have to pretend to be something I wasn't. It wasn't anyone's business who I fucked, was it? Damn it. I hated hiding, but in life, you did what you had to do.

I strolled down the street and looked in the windows on the way back to the hotel. A football game playing on a large screen television caught my eye, and I got a lump in my throat. I heard my mother's voice in my head.

It's your way out, boy — a scholarship, my baby in college. Imagine. It's a dream, Diego.

For what seemed like a second in time, it was all in my hands. I was playing college ball, in college by grace of a football scholarship, and my coach was talking NFL. He'd managed to interest a big-shot recruiter. He was coming to see me play, making a stop on his way to Washington just to see me.

When he sees you play, he'll be blown away. You'll be recruited, playing for the NFL, rolling in dough.

But then my mother called me. The bank was ready to re-possess. She worked as a waitress at a local diner, making just enough to cover the minimum. I'd had to bail her out a few times already. She was hurting; not enough shifts at the restaurant where the owner thought he had exclusive rights to paw the waitresses. I knew one last fight would do it.

When I was a kid, I worked every day after school, doing whatever I could to help out. My father had left us high and dry, and my mother was Creole, the descendant of an Afri-can slave and a white slave owner. Her café au lait skin and lack of education made it hard for her to find work that paid decently. When I was fourteen, I got a job working for a mobster who ran an underground extreme fight network. Anything went, and sometimes the men fought to the death while people took bets on who'd be left standing. He paid me well, mostly to keep my mouth shut and run errands. I'd seen fighters beaten to death with lead pipes and dumped in the bayou to be gobbled up by the gators, but I'd also seen the amount of money the one left standing could make. I wanted in. I was tough, big for my age, and fast. I'd won two contests before the age of eighteen.

I came home from college on the weekend and arranged to fight on Saturday night. My mother begged me not to go.

Diego, that guy from the NFL is coming to see you play next week. You won't be able to play football, impress that big-shot re-cruiter. I've seen you hurt for days after one of those fights. Please, son, don't do it.

But they were going to take her house away, and they were coming on Tuesday. The house was all she had. If she didn't make the payment, she'd be in the street. This fight would pay ten-thousand dollars to the man left standing. It would be enough. I'd won before, and I'd win this time.

And I did win. I saved my mother's house. I came away with several broken bones, though, and I was too beaten up to show up for the game. My one chance to be recruited to the big leagues was gone, and the doctors told me that my days of being able to run like the wind were over. My legs would heal but running for long periods of time would result in pain.

I fell into despair. I drank and took drugs to forget, and before I knew it, I'd turned into my father. I fought in one fight after another to help my mother and pay the drug dealers fueling my habit. The debts to the dealers kept climbing.

I knew the Banni was often present at those fights, but I didn't know that Chase had been following my so-called career, had bet, and made a fortune on my purses.

The drug dealers threatened to kill me, and Chase assumed my debts. He paid them off and then grabbed me and took me to his cabin in the woods. He gave me a choice. He said, get clean and join the club or die.

Six years later, here I was, doing the big fight a few times a year, and pounding face for Chase and the Banni. Was I happy? No. I was resigned, just like I'd been resigned to the fact that my father was a dirty coward who'd deserted his wife and son, and that I'd never have a career in football like I dreamed I would. Life sucks. So what? That's why you needed to take what pleasure you could and never apologize for it.

My mother was disappointed in me for becoming a member of the Banni. I knew that. She never wanted to take the money I gave her, so I had to pay her bills for her. I paid off the house. I gave the grocery store a tab in my name, on my credit card. I sent payments in her name to every utility. She knew, of course, but she couldn't protest that way. But she'd still refused to see me for a long time. Then one day, I had someone call her up and offer her a job answering phones and such at Banni Scrap Yard. The salary and benefits were excellent. She had no idea I was one of the owners until she showed up. At this point, she forgave me and took the job. Love and money were the two most powerful motivators in the world.

I know this is not what she wanted for me. Perhaps she'd blamed herself, but there was no one to blame except maybe for that Cajun bastard that sired me. Things were the way they were. Now, like my ma, I was resigned to my lot in life.

And the Banni were my family now. Chase had saved me in more ways than one and I owed him, even if he got on my last nerve sometimes.

However, that didn't mean Chase needed to know who I took to my bed. And tonight, he wouldn't.

The doorman opened the door for me as I walked into the lobby of the swanky hotel. I strode right up to this snooty-looking guy behind the desk and said. "Good evening. Suite four, please, a Mr. Colby Young."

"Who shall I say is calling, sir?"

"Diego," I said.

"Does Diego have a last name?"

What a snob. "Just say Diego," I told him.

"Just a moment." The man picked up the phone and waited. Then he said, "Mr. Young, there is a . . . well . . . Diego, here at the front desk, without a last name." He looked at me. "Yes, sir," he said, hanging up.

"I'll escort you to the elevator," he said, looking down his nose at me. "We lock them for security reasons promptly at six p.m."

I smiled. He probably wanted to add "to keep out the likes of you," but he didn't. Instead, he slid a keycard into the slot, and the elevator opened. He leaned over and pressed something, then held the elevator open for me. "Mr. Young is expecting you."

"Thanks," I said, taking a one hundred dollar bill out of

my wallet and passing it to him. "For your trouble."

His mouth opened. I admit I had a hard time keeping a straight face.

I stepped into the elevator and the doors closed. I loved doing exactly the opposite of what people expected of me. I'd always been like that.

I watched the elevator rise, and I sobered. I wasn't sure what I was getting into here, but, like Colby Young, I was up for a little intrigue. The elevator dinged and opened onto a full-sized suite.

My boots sank into a plush blue carpet as I swept the large room, equipped with royal blue velvet colonial-style furniture. There was a giant flat-screen television on one wall and a huge oil painting of brightly colored flowers in a vase on the other.

A stereo was playing some Elton John tune from his latest CD, and I noticed there was a half tumbler of something smoky sitting on a glass coffee table.

Directly in front of me were windows that spanned from floor to ceiling, affording a beautiful view of downtown Austin and the Colorado River.

I walked through the room. I picked up the glass and sniffed it. Brandy. The good stuff. I went over to the window and stood there, looking out.

"What took you so long?"

I could see his reflection in the glass, dressed in one of those unflattering terry robes hotels like this provided to their guests.

I turned around. "Wasn't sure I was coming."

"Oh," he said. "You're going to come." He undid the tie on his robe and pushed it off. He stood there stark naked. "I'll meet you in the bedroom."

I was a little stumped. What, no drink? No small talk? I grinned and followed him. I liked his style.

Artificial Moonlight

The bedroom was no less impressive than the living room. More plush carpets, a gigantic round bed with lots of cushions. I was pretty sure the sheets had a high thread count—and of course, duvets.

The lamps were on, and I could see him clearly. He propped himself up on his elbow and met my gaze. "So, take 'em off, unless you're scared."

I smiled. "You keep insinuating that I'm scared," I told him, pulling off my T-shirt. "Should I be?"

He sat up straight. "Jesus," he said softly. He came off the bed and reached out to trail his fingers over my ribcage. "Faded bruises. Where'd you get those?"

"Courtesy of a baseball bat in a redneck bar back home."

He looked up at me. "Those guys still walking?"

"They will . . ." I smiled faintly. "Eventually."

He met my gaze in such an intense way. I felt my knees grow weak. I wet my lips. He placed a hand on my chest, moved it across my pectorals then over my biceps. He stepped back. "You are incredible."

I reached out for him, but he crawled back on the bed. He propped pillows under his head. "Go on."

I frowned. "What is this?"

"I'm trying to prolong the pleasure. You realize this is a one-night thing. When it's one night only, well . . ."

I was growing frustrated. I kicked off my boots and un-zipped my pants. I was standing there in my briefs when he said. "You'd be perfect."

I narrowed my eyes. "Perfect for what?"

"I'll tell you later." He rolled over onto his stomach and rummaged in the drawer. I saw him take out condoms and lube. "I want to . . ." he began, but I didn't wait for him to finish. I'd had enough of show and tell.

I went over to the bed and reached for him. I caught his ankle and pulled him down to the end. He glanced up at me with fire in his eyes. He looked like he was about to protest.

I took his ass-cheeks in my hands and massaged them, nudging his thighs apart with my knee as I crawled on the bed. My other hand reached for his hair, and I pulled his head up and met his gaze. "You want to fuck or what?"

"Think you can handle me?"

"I'm pretty sure of it," I said. I was horny as hell. I dropped his head and pulled him up onto his knees. Spreading his ass, I began to slowly rim him.

I could tell he didn't expect that. He let out a cry and wiggled a little. I held him fast, my tongue jabbing up inside of him as he moaned. Then I reached around and took hold of his dick, squeezing and jerking. He was hard, already dripping pre-come.

If he was expecting a fast, hard fuck from some horny biker, he was in for a surprise. My specialty was being able to predict what people expected I'd do, then do something completely different. That's how come I wasn't lying at the bottom of the bayou, being some gator's midnight snack. I was in for the night, and I intended to enjoy every moment. And if he wasn't in seventh heaven, then neither would I be.

I never understood how anyone could be turned on by rape, gaining pleasure from someone's body when they clearly didn't want you inside them.

I wanted Colby to want me. In fact, I wanted him to beg for it. It was clear as I held him fast, and kept rimming and fondling him, that he loved the fact that I could handle him, make him submit.

I got off the bed and came over to the side. Colby looked at me with lust in his eyes. I rolled him over onto his back and pulled him to the side of the bed, tilting his head back. "Suck it," I told him, wiping my cock over his lips. Colby opened his mouth and took it inside, while I ran a hand over his chest and stiffened his nipples.

His hips lifted as he sucked, and I pulled him over sideways some so I could reach his cock. He was moaning as he licked and slurped on my shaft, taking me into his throat. I cried out something. Jesus. I fondled his cock and his balls as he continued. I was going to come. I jerked back and took my cock in hand. I slammed into the wall and let it take me.

Colby's hands on me reminded me I wasn't alone. He grabbed my neck and pulled my head down for a kiss as his hands roamed my body with abandon. He took my hand and led me back to the bed, pushing me onto my back. He crawled on top and leaned down to lick my chest slowly. I moved my hands over his back, his ass. His mouth crashed down on mine again, and I rolled over on him, my lips moving down the length of him.

I took his cock in my mouth, and again I heard him gasp. To suck cock was definitely a giving activity. Maybe he thought I wouldn't do that. I was on my knees on the floor, his legs hanging over and I sucked him deep in my throat, taking in his balls, one at a time.

I felt his fingers curl in my hair and pull. He cried out, and his semen gushed into my mouth. I took it, swallowed some, spit some. I wiped my mouth, my cock hard again. I looked down at him. "I'm going to fuck you now, on your knees, real dirty."

He reached up, grabbed me by the hair, and pulled me onto the bed. He got on top of me. "Damn, you're pretty. You're too damn pretty." He grasped my shaft in his hand, and I grunted. "Fuck me then. Do your best, but be forewarned, it's hard to please me. Real hard."

I smiled at him and pushed him onto the floor. "Is that so? Well, let's see if I can ruin your record. I'm hard enough." I grabbed him rough and yanked him to his knees. I pushed his head down. I smacked his ass a few times and checked his cock. Hard, real hard. The key was to keep him hard while I fucked him and then get him to come just as I pulled out. My mouth moved up beside his ear. I kissed it lightly. "Are you a whore? If you weren't before, you are to-night, Colby. You're my whore."

I checked his cock. Oh yeah. His cock liked that. He liked to know I could handle him, please him, and tease him. He liked the dirty talk, and right now, by the way he was breathing, he liked being forced to his knees like this, his ass in the air.

I ran my hands over his spine, put some kisses there, slapped his ass a few times. Each time he tried to pick up his head, I pushed it down. I wouldn't hurt him, but I let him know there was no escape. That was exciting him. I rubbed his nipples. They were peaks of stiffness. Sensitive, too. He moaned like a whore each time I pulled and rolled them between my fingers.

I lubed my fingers, and I jabbed two of them into his ass. He cried out, but it was from pleasure. I pushed them deeper inside of him and lowered my lips to his ear. "Nice ass, nice and tight, perhaps too tight for my cock. You're going to feel it, baby. I'll make sure of that. Your ass is my playground tonight."

Colby jerked under me, hissed in some breath. I heard him say "please" as I fucked his ass with two, then three, fingers. I reached under and fondled his balls, rubbed his nipples, lifted my other hand and stuck my finger in his mouth. He sucked on it as I withdrew my fingers from his ass.

I pulled him up straight in my arms and pressed my cock against his ass. He was trembling all over. "Am I dangerous enough for you, Colby?"

There was a full-length mirror there, and I looked at us in the mirror, my face beside his, one hand rubbing his nipples, the other playing lightly with his cock. He bucked into me, his head lolling back.

"Please," he pleaded.

"Please what?" I asked, holding his cock in my hand. "You're so hot, so ready. Look at you, the sweat running down your chest. What a beautiful slut you are, Colby. Want me?"

He grunted. "God, yes. Yes."

I spread his ass and pushed him forward. "Watch yourself getting fucked," I told him.

I slipped on the condom and plunged my cock into his ass. He let out a wail, and I spanked him lightly. "God, you feel so . . . good," I grunted. He did. The best ass I'd ever had the pleasure of taking. I looked up before I really started to pound him, and he was watching us in the mirror. There was a smile on his face. I gave it to him. I fucked so hard and so long, holding on as much as I could. Then, as I came, I pulled him up into my arms, bit lightly into his shoulder, and jerked him to completion. Our chests heaved as the sound of our rapid breathing filled the room and bounced off the walls.

We stayed there on our knees, Colby resting in my arms for the longest time. Our sweat-soaked bodies glistening in the lamplight as Colby turned his face to mine and tenderly kissed my lips, caressing my long hair as he did.

I kissed him back, pulling him around to face me as my hands slid down his back to his ass.

After a while, I sat back on the carpet while he stayed upright on his knees, his gaze moving over me. He didn't say anything. What could we say after that?

Colby got to his feet after a few minutes. He walked out of the room while I stayed there on the floor. When he didn't come back, I figured that was my cue to leave. I wondered if he'd let me take a shower.

I got to my feet and walked out into the living room. He

stood there, looking out at the lights, wrapped in that hotel robe again. "Hey," I said.

He turned and looked at me. "Wanna drink?"

I shook my head. "Think I could use the shower?"

"Sure." He turned back to the window.

Guess he wasn't in the talkative mood. That was okay. I found the bathroom and took a quick shower. When I came out, Colby was there, handing me a towel. He let his gaze wander over me in that way he had of inspecting me in a most intimate way. He did it even when I was dressed.

I wound one towel around my waist and began to towel dry my hair with another. When I put the towel aside, Colby picked up a hairbrush. "Let me."

I shrugged.

He began to brush my hair. "It's beautiful," he said.

I smiled. "Thanks."

He led me to a stool in the bathroom. "I can't reach." He laughed.

I nodded and sat down.

"So . . ." He began brushing, looking in the mirror. "How tall are you anyway?"

"Six-six."

"That's tall." He smiled.

"You don't have to do this, you know. I can leave."

"Without breakfast?" He lifted an eyebrow.

Damn, he was hard to figure. He obviously wasn't a cuddler, and he wasn't into much conversation after sex either, but he seemed to be enjoying the hair brushing.

"Want to let it dry naturally, or I could use the dryer."

"What are you, a hairdresser?" I laughed.

"No." He put down the brush.

"So what is it you do?"

"Work for my father."

"Who has a lot of dough."

26

"Right. Actually, you'd be perfect for a commercial he's doing. It's for . . . you know who . . . the king of motorcycles?"

"No thanks," I said, standing. "I'm no model. Besides, the club wouldn't like it. We keep a low profile."

Colby nodded.

"So," I said as we walked out into the living room, "did I measure up? You said you were hard to please."

He met my gaze. "Is that what's important to you?"

"It seemed to be important to you, since you told me about it just before I was about to fuck you."

"Didn't seem to hurt your performance any."

"I take that as a positive critique."

He shrugged. "Take it any way you want." He looked at me. "We understand each other, right?"

"I guess," I said. Frankly, I understood nothing about Colby Young except that he had a rich dad, was pretty fussy when it came to sex, and he seemed to run a bit hot and cold.

"I usually don't fuck the same guy twice. It's a rule."

"Really?" I looked at him. "And what's that all about?"

"I don't want to get involved. I want to have fun, experience pleasure, variety. That's all."

"So I was the perfect choice."

"Does that bother you?"

"No," I replied.

"You don't feel used, do you?" He laughed.

Fuck. "Since you put it that way."

He looked at me. "So, you riding in the parade?"

"Yes."

"Me, too. I'm sure I'll see you there. I have a great bike."

"I'm sure you do. You have a great car."

"Not mine. Jerry's."

"Oh, Jerry is your friend?"

"My best friend. Jerry lives part-time here in Austin. My

bike's at his place. You could ride by and take a look at it if you want to. Jerry's interested in doing you, too, if you're into it. You'll be here the entire four days, right?"

Nothing much shocks me, but Colby's words rendered me speechless. I'd just finished having mind-blowing sex with this guy, and he was passing me off to his buddy? "You're kidding, right?"

He wasn't looking at me. He didn't answer for a minute.

"Colby?" I walked over to him and turned him around. "What do you think I am, some stud for hire you can pass around to your jet set?"

"I'm sorry if you took it that way. I was only saying it wouldn't bother me."

I moved closer and put my hands on either side of his face. I met his gaze. "And why is it so important to you that I know that? Who are you trying to convince?"

He tried to struggle away. "Don't get too high on yourself."

"Oh, no worries. Won't happen around you."

"What are you doing?" He looked nervous, still trying to wiggle free. "We won't do this again. Once. It's my rule. I told you."

I leaned in and kissed him hard. At first, he tried to pull away, then he surrendered. I felt his arms move up around my neck, fingers in my hair. I reached in to undo the sash on his robe. I wanted him again. I took his cock in my hand. It was already hard. I squeezed it gently.

He moaned.

I pulled my mouth away. "You say one thing, but your cock says another."

Anger sparked in his eyes, and he gave me a solid push away. "I think you should leave now, Diego." He turned his back again.

I felt like shit. "I was leaving. Don't worry. I have no

problem with your stupid rule. Once with you is more than enough. I'll get my clothes." I went into the bedroom and got dressed. I took one look at the bed and the place on the floor where I'd fucked him. I could see the indentations in the carpet, could still smell the sex. I closed my eyes for a second before I walked back out into the living room.

Colby was looking out the window again. I knew he could see my reflection. He didn't speak, so I pressed the elevator button. I didn't say goodbye.

When the elevator doors opened, Colby turned around and looked at me. He said my name. I looked away and let the doors separate us. My heart was pounding hard. I wasn't sure why, but I felt as if I'd been on a roller coaster ride, a ride I never wanted to get on again.

CHAPTER THREE

Colby

A few hours later, I watched the sun rise as I looked out of the hotel room window and studied the motorbikes crammed on either side of Sixth Street. The locals had come out to gawk at some of the fanciest hogs I've ever seen. Whole families crowded around rides so huge and gaudily painted that I found it embarrassing to be even remotely associated with them.

All the way from here, I could pick out Spider's signature Harley. That custom piece was hot—a big, platinum spider. He coveted that thing like a lover. I couldn't resist smirking. I preferred something a lot softer between my legs.

I had to get ready, but I couldn't get moving.

I felt bad sending Diego away like that.

But I had to.

There was something about Diego that was strong and sweet. "Sweet, like a Texas peach," my daddy would have said. People would ask, "Don't you mean a Georgia peach?" That was the common expression.

"No," he'd respond. "A Texas peach." To him, it was the most delicious, forbidden fruit. My mama came from Texas—Stonewall, actually. Her folks owned a peach farm there, and my dad had ridden by it on his way from Louisiana to Texas with his as-yet-unnamed motorcycle gang about thirty years ago now.

They'd arrived early for the bike rally here in Austin and

heard there was a rodeo in Stonewall, a well . . . stone's throw from the music capital, about sixty-three miles, to be exact. His hog broke down right past the farm, so he strolled back onto the property and asked the farmer if he had some tools he could borrow. The farmer was understandably frightened when he saw six leather-jacketed bikers crowding around him, but my dad, Cledus Young, was a Southern boy, and he poured on the charm.

Born and raised in St John the Baptist parish back in Louisiana, he was respectful. He eased the farmer's anxieties with his smooth talk and infectious smile.

Besides—my daddy told me—he'd just gotten his first glimpse of the farmer's daughter. Nothing but dirty thoughts on his mind after that. He was already marrying her and knocking her up in his heart and head.

The story he told me was that she was sitting in a rocking chair on the porch with a bowl of rock salt on one side, sliced peaches on the other, mixing a batch of homemade ice cream by hand.

He fell in love on the spot.

So did she.

Evangeline was a blonde, blue-eyed beauty, who would become Stonewall's Peach Queen six months later when she turned eighteen. My pa, the dark-haired, brooding type, had by then taken a summer job in the farm's canning house in exchange for the opportunity to use the farmer's tools to work on his bike. He stayed and stayed, working on Evangeline's daddy something fierce to earn the right to marry her.

It was like something out of a fairy tale.

Except fairy tales have happy endings.

I walked into the bathroom and showered. I was gonna visit the old farm after the bike rally was over. Then I'd head back home.

I could still smell Diego on my skin. I had to quit thinkin' about him. I had other things on my mind. Family things.

And I don't believe in happy endings.

I turned the hot water on, hot as I could stand it, and wished the river of heat would block the old memories.

What had I expected, coming back to where it all began?

My heart gave a lurch under the torture, and I braced my hands on the shower wall, trying to let the searing, liquid fire soak through me.

What won my granddaddy over in the end was that he learned my pa was a descendant of John Young, a man who was initially taken hostage by the Hawaiian king, Kamehameha the Great, more than two hundred years ago.

This was right after Captain Cook blundered badly with the natives, taxing their hospitality. He got himself killed—not that John Young and his shipmates knew this. When their merchant ship pulled into Kealakekua Bay on the Big Island, the king, fed up with foreign visitors, snatched John Young the moment he touched dry land.

John Young used his own charm to talk to the king. Very quickly, he became his most trusted advisor.

I had to grin. Kinda like me and Spider, really.

Soaping up, I wished I'd been born and raised in Hawaii instead of the South. My great, great, great, great Uncle John had married himself a Hawaiian princess. My pa never talks about that side of the family much. Guess we're too removed. We don't live like royal descendants and have nothing to show for our connections to Hawaiian kings and princesses. Never have. Never will.

Ma might have been beautiful, but she was demented. Pa told me he was hopelessly in love with her before he realized just how nuts she was. He had no way of knowing that he'd met her on a good day when she was so hopped up—unknowingly—on Vistaril, an anti-psychotic medication her dad was able to successfully hide in peach tea and ice cream.

Even skipping a dose proved disastrous. Off the medication, Evangeline was fond of talking to herself, removing her clothes, and running down the street naked. And oh, yeah, lashing out at her father, and later, my pa, with her hands and venomous words. But still, Cledus married her.

"It's because of the crazy sex," he once confessed to me. "Crazy girls fuck best, boy. It's unbeatable. Don't ever let anyone tell you any different."

I think I inherited her genes. I'm kinda partial to crazy sex myself. I've inherited her sexual appetite and her blue eyes. I've inherited my pa's moodiness and his dark hair. I hope I haven't inherited Evangeline's insanity, though. I got enough problems as it is. She and my pa married, and in a very short time had me, then my two sisters.

June came a year after me. She was named after the June Gold peach, one of the most popular varieties in the Texas hill country. Last, but not least, was baby Garnet, also named for a peach. The Garnet Beauty.

I rinsed off quickly. Damn it. Why did I have to think about her? I swiped a towel off the heated rung. Nice and warm. I began to dry off.

My parents fought constantly in their time together, and by the time I was five, June was four, and Garnet was two, my ma left my pa. Evangeline took the girls. Cledus took me.

I thought I had it rough living with my grief-stricken father, but things didn't sound fun with Evangeline, and the girls in the rare phone conversations pa and I had with them. Cledus and I rarely spoke to the girls, and Evangeline just yelled a lot, refusing to see us. She said crap like all men were rapists. Cledus never pushed the issue. When she started ranting, he'd hang up fast.

By then, he had a secret world he never spoke about. He grew distant and angry.

Turns out he wasn't the only one with secrets. Something

went terribly wrong with my ma, and by the time I ran away from home to find my sisters, I was twelve, June Gold was eleven, and Garnet Beauty was . . . gone.

My mom and sisters had moved to East Baton Rouge in the Florida parishes and lived in a crumbly house with household help, but nobody could explain what had happened to Garnet, who should have been nine. June wept and said she had vanished three years before.

"I'm not allowed to talk about her," she said. "All her things are gone."

June Gold had kept one little dress that had belonged to Garnet Beauty. I remembered it. June still has it. It's lilac-colored with tiny grapes and pink lilacs on it. It's faded now, the fruit and flowers indistinct. Sometimes she takes it out and just holds it, to remind herself that our Garnet was real. She had been alive. And she had been an absolute beauty.

How did a mother lose a child and just pretend she never existed?

My ma just got angry when I made a fuss, and my pa, when he showed up after I called him, could get no sense out of her.

I got a whipping as soon as Cledus walked through the door. I didn't care. I just wanted him to find my sister. He'd had no idea Garnet had disappeared. After beating the crap out of me, he called the police.

My mother had never reported Garnet missing, but the police began to chase up the story. My mother claimed to have left the girls in the care of her boyfriend at the time, while she was at work. She said she thought he'd kidnapped her. She had no pictures of her, having destroyed them all because she said she couldn't bear to look at her, but June had kept one. It had been taken when Garnet was five, and goddamn it, she looked just like me, except her hair was long.

The police took the photo, making my sister cry. That and the dress were all she had of Garnet girl.

"Did you look for her?" the police asked Evangeline. "Did you even try?"

She just wound her long, flyaway hair around her index finger and hummed. By then, June Gold was taking care of Evangeline, who was now on a heady mixture of Lithium and Xanax.

Nobody was taking care of me.

I wanted to grab my sister and go to our granddaddy's farm. I was certain life would be fairer to us there.

There was a TV show on the air at the time called Unsolved Mysteries. They did a segment about our sister. Nothing ever came of it. That was fifteen years ago. My heart still aches for Garnet Beauty. June and I will never be the same without her. I won't rest until we find her—one way or another—but I haven't, and won't ever, talk to my mom again.

June Gold got married young. Too young. She was sixteen and badly wanted to escape our mother. Evangeline went into assisted living. I haven't seen her since. June tortures herself with occasional visits, in which Evangeline either doesn't know her or rips June a new one for putting her in, what I am told, is a pretty decent facility.

My dad pays for it. He can afford it.

June and I moved to New Orleans after Hurricane Katrina. I opened my own pool hall and gave June the money to open a bakery. She's a fantastic cook, and I'd put her through culinary school with money I earned working two jobs.

She wanted to specialize in Mardi Gras king cakes, but I thought it might be a once-a-year kind of business. Then she met Judd, an okay guy if ever I met one. Judd bakes, too. They proved me wrong. Apparently, the world loves Mardi Gras. And, it seems, king cakes. She bakes from recipes handed down from my pa's family. She ships internationally and I am mighty proud of how well she's doing. She sends her worldwide customers frothy cakes in boxes stuffed with Mardi Gras beads and porcelain masks. As an extra incentive, she includes a bag of local coffee and a few pieces of seasonal fruit.

But no peaches.

Neither of us likes peaches.

June and Judd have two kids, the only ones I'll ever have. There's my niece, Garnet, now four, and nephew, Henry, two, who was named after my maternal grandpa. I love those kids, more than I care to admit. June's a fantastic mother and, so far, the Evangeline curse seems to have skipped two generations of women in our family.

Baby Garnet reminds me of her namesake.

I want, more than anything, to bring my sister home. I want to run like the wind with her. I want to count snails on stone walls like we used to as kids. I want to hug her and hide her from any more pain.

Is she dead or alive?

The police detective who caught our case stays in touch with me, and he's as hopeful as I. Sometimes he despairs, too. He never contacts June Gold, who falls apart when Detective Duchesne talks to her. My dad never returns his calls, so Duchesne calls me.

Sometimes, he finds a dead girl and lets me know they haven't forgotten Garnet Beauty. Sometimes it hurts like fuck when he gets my hopes up, only to crush them again. He found a living girl one time and said he thought it could be my sister. I went to meet her, but it wasn't.

I felt like one of Cinderella's stepsisters and finally understood why they tried so hard to make that glass shoe fit. I badly wanted the amnesiac girl in the hospital to be Garnet, except her eyes were mud-brown and she turned out to be a fugitive from Ireland, who never expected all the publicity she got.

So all of that is why I sent Diego out the door. He makes me think of ripe peaches that smell like candy and drip juice down your chin. As a kid, I loved that. Not anymore.

He makes me want to hope. And I can't.

Hope hurts.

With Garnet Beauty hovering like a sad, tiny specter, I can't enjoy the very thing that brought my parents together.

Love and peaches weren't enough to hold them together, and, I confess, I'd always wanted to believe in the forever kind of love. It still broke my heart that it really didn't exist.

I dried off and dressed in jeans, boots, a shirt, and put on my favorite silver belt buckle.

June made me promise I'd go to the farm since I was coming out here. I don't know why. My grandpa sold the place to another family years ago. When my pa got custody of me, he kept me from my maternal grandpa. I liked the old guy, and Henry's instincts about my pa had been right all along.

But he was gone, long gone. My grandma went before him. It took my pa a couple of years to realize that madness ran in Evangeline's family. Her ma, confined to a sanatorium, went crazy right after she gave birth. So did my ma, except she kept having kids.

She hated me and only wanted girls. After having Garnet, she stopped sleeping with my pa, then wondered why he ran around on her.

I think June Gold, like I, hopes that Garnet might have inherited our ma's fragile mental health and that I'll find her on our granddaddy's front porch making ice cream.

We wish for that more than some kind of nightmare kidnapping . . . torture. Murder.

But like I said, I don't believe in happy endings.

I walked up to Sixth Street, a little nervous about seeing Spider again. He could always tell when I'd got laid and liked to tease me about it. He was the leader of Death Proof, the motorcycle gang I'd joined when I was sixteen. It hadn't been difficult getting in, considering my dad was one of the founding members. He'd always kept that part of his life private, but Evangeline had known about it. Apparently, it was the thing they argued about all the time.

That, and his heavy drinking.

And, of course, her completely irrational outbursts.

He was meaner than a cut snake when he was drunk, and that was from Friday night until Monday morning, when he would go to work at his motorbike and RV dealership. He specialized in travel trailers and motor homes. He promoted family-style RVs and actually sold some of the first luxury fifth wheelers in Louisiana. I thought it was kind of ironic, considering our fractured family life. He worked long days, but his off-duty hours were a mystery to me.

One hellish, cold winter, I had bronchitis. I wanted to be home in my bed, but pa wouldn't allow it.

I wasn't a latchkey kid. He wouldn't give me the key. Not that we needed it. The latch was broken, and my father had developed a fearsome reputation in our parish. Nobody wanted to mess with him.

But I wasn't allowed inside the house until he came home. It took me years to understand that he was worried that his enemies would know I was home alone and kidnap and kill me. He'd already lost one kid, and as much as he liked to take his frustrations out on me, he did love me. In that distant kind of way of his.

So, growing up, I had to hang out on the streets until he showed up. Even when he did, there was never enough food or washing powder.

I am now obsessed with both.

One night I followed him after he claimed to have a business meeting. I was so sick with a raging fever he caved in and let me stay home alone. I figured the meeting must have been important. I itched to know what was really going on, so I followed him on my skateboard. I was pretty fast on that thing and soon witnessed something I now wish I'd never seen. He had a meeting all right, but the brutal fight I witnessed from behind the thick branches of a juniper bush made me realize he was some sort of gang enforcer.

The idea both terrified and thrilled me.

He and a few other guys I'd never seen before met up on the corner of Elm and West Fifth Streets. I watched them park their bikes and walk down the street. I remember my dad holding his helmet in his hand. He swung it from his fingertips in a way I took to be menacing. I kept my gaze on it as I followed them on foot. They disappeared down an alleyway, and next thing I knew, a guy in a black SUV was trying to drive off.

A woman sat beside him in the front seat, screaming. Cledus and his friends surrounded the vehicle. I was so frightened I peed my pants watching my pa smash open the driver's side of the window by using the helmet as a weapon. He dragged the man from the window, the poor guy kicking and screaming. Cledus threw the guy to the ground, he and the others stomping him relentlessly. They only stopped when they heard the sounds of sirens. The guy's wife had crouched down in the front seat and called 911.

As Cledus and the others charged down the alleyway to outrun the cops, he caught me snooping. He grabbed me by the hair, then pulled me out onto the street, where he beat me, too — though not as hard as the guy he'd thrown around in the alley — and left me in a crumpled heap.

"Take it easy," one of the guys yelled, stepping in between us. He was a tall, gangly man, deceptively strong. His intervention enraged my father.

"Fuck off, Calvin!" Cledus shoved the guy back. "He's my kid. I'll beat him to death if I fucking want to!"

Calvin looked shocked. "Jesus," he said. I learned much later that he was the gang's road captain. "You're hurtin' your own kid like that? You really are fucked up, Cledus. You know that?"

They jumped into their own brawl, Calvin finally putting a stop to things. They retreated to separate trees, right there on the street, evidently oblivious to the sounds of sirens roaring away from the alleyway we'd left a few minutes earlier.

After Cledus calmed down some, he pointed to me. "Now yer can quit gripin' and make yerself useful."

I started in the club as a hang around that night, quickly building up to a prospect within a couple of months. Death Proof had a fearsome reputation, yet people like Tony Collins, the guy in the SUV, were so desperate, they would borrow money from the club, with often dire consequences.

Tony had been paying off a five-thousand-dollar loan. Missing one payment proved costly to Tony, who wound up paralyzed, thanks to the beating he took. I followed the story in the newspapers and was surprised when two minor gang members took the rap for it. The club paid their families' expenses, and both guys rose to prominence in the club once they were released. One of them was Punch McGraw, who, first day back in the building, demanded that his son, Jerry, nicknamed Spider, be allowed to join.

Death Proof operated a pool hall with a tatty bar on one side and pool tables on the other. There was always a haze of tobacco smoke over everything, even when the place was supposedly closed. The club had a secret meeting room upstairs. My dad was Death Proof's sergeant at arms and oversaw the bar, which he ruled with an iron fist. My job was to empty ashtrays and wash beer glasses, but even though my tasks were menial, I was treated with a little fear, because of my father's off-kilter personality.

He had a couple of girlfriends, but I began to think he was gay. There were a couple of prospects he seemed to like. He always seemed to go soft on them, especially Jerry. Whereas, if I dropped a cigarette butt on the floor, there was hell to pay.

About six months after I became a prospect, I caught Cledus leaving the club just as I was arriving. He had such a furtive look on his face, I felt compelled to follow him. He rode off on his motorbike, and I urged Jerry, who'd just arrived, driving his mom's car, to follow him. Jerry was a rising prospect, like me. The car was huge—an ancient Impala. It barely kept up with Cledus, but we caught him in the driveway of the shabby Tropic Star Motel.

Jerry freaked out. "We shouldn't be doing this."

"Turn around," I said.

Jerry passed the motel, then turned. We idled kitty-corner, lights extinguished on the vehicle, as we watched Cledus talk with Calvin.

"That's funny," Jerry said. "He and Calvin can't stand each other. Wonder what they're up to?"

Calvin stayed outside, smoking a cigarette, leaning against a dilapidated, fake totem pole, half-hidden as my pa went into the office. He returned with a key. Jerry and I watched their quick, exchanged smiles and then they slipped into a motel room.

Holy shit.

My legs trembled as I got out of the car for a closer look.

Jerry stayed behind the wheel, inching closer to the motel in case we needed to make a quick getaway. Pa and Calvin closed the Venetian blinds, but the blinds were broken. The lower left corner didn't go all the way down. I could see light and movement from inside the room. I don't know what I thought I'd see when I reached the window. I waited several minutes before making my way to the corner and crouching down to look.

The impassioned sounds my pa and Calvin were making should have been a tip-off, but I had to see for myself. There they were in bed. A naked Calvin was lying on his belly, ass in the air, as my father fucked him at a relentless pace. It looked like it hurt, but Calvin looked over his shoulder, saying over and over again, "Give it to me. Harder, man. Fuck you. Harder."

It shocked me.

I got up and walked away. I was turned on, which worried me more than anything. I'd always suspected I was more attracted to men than women but feared my father's wrath. Now I knew the truth. The apple hadn't fallen far from the gay tree.

Jerry was the only one who knew — the only one I told. He confessed to being gay as well, and soon we were exploring each other's bodies in his secret childhood cubby house. It was filled with old comic books and brown recluse spiders. He loved those nasty critters and they, in turn, seemed to appreciate him. But I now had some place to go after school. And the next time my pa tried to put a hand to me, I cautioned him.

"I know about you and that faggot boyfriend of yours. You touch me again, Cledus, and I'll tell everyone in the club that you're a homo."

He looked so shocked that, for one scary moment, I thought he'd put me into an early grave. I noticed a small gleam in his eye. Respect? Maybe. I'd stood up for myself. He and Calvin would go on to continue balling in secret. Publicly, they became president and vice president and still bickered in front of the others. My father is now an inactive lifetime member, and Calvin is the club treasurer. Cledus had to take a less active role, though he finances the club in every way possible. With sixteen vehicle franchises to his credit, plus shares in a couple of custom bike-building shops, he can't do everything. Money and Calvin own his heart and cock. He's basically happy, and so am I.

For a while there, Jerry and I thought we could make a go of it, but I chafed under the possessive constraints of our relationship. He, in turn, couldn't handle what he called my "unavailability."

He's the president, and I'm the road captain, though I find at times that we are compared unfavorably with former regimes because we don't beat people to a pulp. I've never forgotten what Cledus did to Tony Collins, who is still wheelchair-bound. Being a hard man is one thing. Being an uncontrollable lunatic is another.

It's just not me.

As for Jerry, he's found a woman to marry because he says he wants kids. She lives out here in Austin. She owns a tomato farm, of all things, and runs a successful 'green' canning operation. He keeps a lot of his bikes out here on her property — no idea why. She knows he's in a gang, but probably has no idea to what extent. He brought my bike out here in a truck last time he visited because I was having problems with it and he wanted something to do while he was playing happy families with Teresa.

They're getting married in the spring, but I see him already bored and anxious. I wonder if he shuts his eyes when he balls her.

As I turned the corner to Sixth, I tried not to think about the way he'd closed his eyes in ecstasy when we fucked. Sometimes I missed being in bed with him. Mostly, I was glad for the breathing room.

The cacophony of music jarred my senses as I flicked glances from one dim entrance of a bar to another. Spider was supposed to text me with his location, but I knew he was close.

Honky tonk, heavy rock, blues, rap, techno, country . . . it all warred for people's attention. And then I saw him. Spider was propping up the front bar in a beer tavern. The place stunk and my boots stuck to the grimy carpet as I stepped inside.

He was dressed head to toe in leather, our gang motif on his back. The grinning skull bore crossed beer bottles instead of bones, and Spider's jacket had the number thirteen dangling from the epaulette, the universal biker symbol for being partial to marijuana.

He seemed to be in an unusually bad mood. I'd never seen Spider mad, except now, as he knocked back beers and tequila chasers like the city was about to run out of both. Two rival gang members I didn't recognize had surrounded him. As I approached, the one closest to me stepped back.

I remembered him now. Butch Miller. He was with some Australian gang with ties to the Texas cattle industry. The annual bike rally brought out all the freaks and weirdoes. Or, as Cledus was fond of saying, "Somebody opens up all the cages."

"G'day," Butch said, like some misdirected extra from a Crocodile Dundee movie.

"Hey, Butch." I nodded an acknowledgment and moved in beside Spider. I realized Spider's anger was all show. His hand shook a little, and I could smell the desperation and fear seeping from his pores. What the hell was going on?

He began drinking another beer, the bartender frantically filling orders as George Strait began bellowing from the sound system.

"So why are you hanging out at gay bars, Jerry?" the other biker asked.

Oh, boy. When had Jerry been inside a gay bar? We

hadn't been in town that long and he supposedly went off to see Teresa and to pick up his bike.

"The Back Room's not gay," Jerry muttered, between sips. He sounded calm, but I knew him well and realized he was in deep shit.

"Your old lady seems to think so. Heard her screamin' at you."

Teresa suddenly appeared from the back of the bar. I assumed she'd been in the can, judging by the alarming height of her blonde hair and the enormous smear of red lipstick across her teeth. Teresa was a pretty woman who wore way too much makeup and always carried a huge purse. I always wondered what the hell she kept in that thing, and I'd occasionally asked Spider if it weighed his bike down at all, but he would never answer the question.

I'd never seen Teresa do anything but smile. Suddenly she swung her purse at him, connecting hard.

"What the . . ." He fell back, almost on top of me.

"How sweet," she snarled, "right in your lover's arms."

The fight was on. Teresa kept swinging wildly, connecting with that fucking purse that felt like it had been weighed down with bricks. I got a flash memory of my pa swinging his helmet and knew she meant to inflict damage.

I couldn't hit a woman. Neither could Spider, and she knew it.

She'd calculated wrongly though if she thought the fight would remain between the three of us. As the Bee Gees took over the sound system, I saw the worried look on the bartender's face. Beer bottles flew, and the Australian idiots jumped all over me and Spider. We punched them back. Spider and I weren't the kinda guys who started trouble, but we sure didn't back away from a fight either. Out of nowhere, I saw a pair of hands grab for Teresa's purse. It flew over the counter and smashed into the mirrored back of the wall, knocking out a row of bottles with it.

A fist slammed into my jaw, and I rocketed back with a few of my own, connecting with somebody's ribs. I heard a sickening crack, even with all the chaos going on around me.

One of the Australians had sunk to the floor. He flicked out a knife, so I kicked him in the head, and he fell flat on his face.

Another fist loomed over me. I heard Teresa screaming, "Faggot!"

A deathly hush fell over everyone as the fist came for me, a knife in its grip.

Spider was on the floor, face down. I could see blood pouring from his mouth, Teresa stomping him. I kicked her foot away from his head. I didn't care if the knife got me. I tried to block the blow coming to me, just as another hand grabbed the fist.

"Fuck!" the man with the knife yelled as the hand clutching his began to bear down, crunching bones in his fingers.

"Drop the knife," a calm voice said.

I drew a breath, tasting blood in my mouth. I glanced at the man who'd saved my life.

Holy crap.

Diego.

CHAPTER FOUR

I'd had no idea the Banni were even in the house.
Diego gave me a look somewhere between a smirk and a smile. I smiled back.

"Thanks," I mumbled, tonguing my teeth to make sure nothing was broken. My lip had been cut, but it could have been worse. Spider was on his knees, coughing and spluttering. Teresa was a weepy mess on the floor.

"What were you doing on Fourth Street?" she screamed.

"Shut up," I said to her. "Just shut up. Not every bar there is gay."

Spider was looking at me. "I think I'm fucked up." He reached a hand under his jacket, and it came away again, covered in blood.

"We'll get you to the hospital." I grabbed keys from his shaky hand, and Diego helped me outside with him.

The cops were arriving, and I'd never been so grateful to see an ambulance in my life. As Diego and I each shouldered Spider to the wagon, the paramedics donned gloves at the first sign of blood. They helped us put Spider on a gurney.

"It hurts bad," he moaned. One of the paramedics cut open Spider's leather vest. He had a deep stab wound to the abdomen, just above his waistband. I knew it was about the most painful injury a man could have.

"Ride with him," Diego said to me. "I'll follow you."

I would have argued, but I figured having the Banni tailing us might prevent any wise guys from a rival group trying to shoot at the ambulance.

"I'm gonna die," Spider moaned as we took off, the sirens wailing.

"No, you're not," I retorted, but the truth was, all the blood pouring from him and his sickeningly pale face worried me. What if he did die? Then I would have lost two people I loved. I couldn't lose Spider and Garnet.

"Stay with me, Jerry," I said. "Don't leave me."

He looked up at me from eyes filled with pain. His oxygen mask bore blood stains that rocked me. Neither of us had ever been seriously hurt in a fight before.

Swallowed his own teeth, the paramedic treating him told me. Geez. Teresa had really gone berserk on him.

At St David's Hospital, the staff was waiting for us, wheeling Spider into the emergency room doors the second the vehicle stopped moving. I was aware of the roar of bikes and turned to see some of our own members there, as well as the Banni.

My gaze connected with Calvin's. He parked his bike off to the side and inclined his head as he got off again.

I followed him.

"What the hell was he doing over on Fourth Street?" he asked me, his voice low.

"No idea." And I didn't. Fourth Street was Austin's barely — their gay district, comprised of Oil Can Harry's — the only durable GLBT-friendly bar — and three others that changed ownership with alarming frequency. One of them, the Back Room, was no longer gay-friendly, but I was beginning to think Spider must have gone to meet someone there, thinking he was safe.

"He didn't tell you?" Calvin had a funny look on his face.

"What is it?" I asked.

"You really don't know?" He looked nervous now.

"No. Obviously, you know something I don't."

He leaned into me, and I could smell Juicy Fruit gum on

his breath. "He was there to meet me."

I gaped at him. Calvin's gaze was so weird it took me a few seconds to realize exactly what he was telling me. He was saying that he and Spider were . . . an item?

"What the fuck?" I was horrified. Not the least because he was supposed to be banging Cledus.

"Are you judging me?" Calvin's face turned gray. I had to remind myself he was no pussycat.

I shook my head. "I'm trying to understand."

"He doesn't have anybody else, and your pa, well, let's just say he has problems and I can't deal with them right now."

"Problems?" The shocks kept coming today. "New ones or the same old?"

"New ones. He has prostate cancer and won't follow all the treatment procedures. Skips his chemo sessions and shit. I ain't gonna sit back and watch that motherfucker die on me. You need to talk to him, Colby. He'll listen to you."

"No, he won't." But I already knew he would. Cledus and I were not close and growing farther apart by the second. And yet, he tried hard to reach out to me constantly. I was having a hard time accepting the nature of Spider and Calvin's relationship, even though my old man was an ass. He didn't deserve the one person he'd been good to cheating on him.

Damn it. I'd have to get home soon and deal with my father.

I turned to find Diego's sympathetic gaze on my face. I had no idea how much he'd heard or what he'd figured out, but I felt seriously depressed. Everything was changing so fast, and I didn't like change. Not at all.

"Thanks," I said to him.

He nodded. "Spider's gone into surgery."

Oh, geez.

A few of my club members sauntered over to me.

"How's he doin'?" seemed to be the recurring question.

Inside the hospital, I got no news. I had to call Spider's mom, who freaked out over the phone.

"I'm flying in," Sue Ellen said. "Did that bitch Teresa have anything to do with this?"

"Um, yeah." I couldn't deny it. Spider's mom had taken care of me my last two years of high school when he and I were particularly close. Sue Ellen may have figured out we were lovers but never said a word. All she cared about was our grades—and our health. She lectured us about condom use and taking vitamins. She made sure we did both. I recall a close relationship with Trojans foil packs and Flintstone gummies in my senior year. No. I couldn't lie to the only woman who'd ever shown me a shred of maternal affection.

"I'm going to kill her," Sue Ellen said.

I had no doubt Spider's mom could get herself into a physical fight with Teresa, especially when provoked. I didn't think, however, that she would come out the winner against Spider's woman. First of all, Sue Ellen is an animal lover. She loves spiders, for chrissakes. She keeps them as pets and frets when they disappear from her living room.

Over the years, they have spun enormous webs so complex and thick that even her dog gets stuck in them. Sue Ellen and Jerry have a thing for spiders, and the rest of us have learned to suffer in silence. Even their dog has learned to lick sticky spider silk from his fur without a whimper.

"I'll pull out every last strand of her fake hair and knit a sweater with it. We've got some elephants at the circus here in town. They could use the warmth."

I almost laughed, except that I half believed her.

"I'm booking a flight now, and I'll be there as soon as possible. I'll call you with my arrival time. You'll pick me up at the airport."

"Yes, ma'am."

She ended the call, and I joined the others as they paced the waiting room. Diego stood against the wall, arms folded, looking sexier than hell. I wondered why the Australian gang had started the fight and realized we'd need to retaliate. Diego and I exchanged weighty glances. I couldn't deal with him right now, much as I wanted to. I thought about how nice it had been tangling in bed. I'd have given anything to turn back time and go right back there.

Just past Diego stood a few more of his gang members. Sometimes when there was a rumble, rival gangs came together. I owed Diego and his crew. I'd never forget that.

Out of the corner of my eye, I caught Calvin gesturing to me. I walked over to him as he slipped around the corner into the hallway.

"Walk with me." His voice was a mere whisper.

I trotted to keep up with him.

"We were set up," he said, as soon as he thought we were safe.

I narrowed my eyes. "What do you mean?"

"I mean, we were set up. I never told Jerry to meet me at the Back Room bar. I'd never put either of us at risk going to openly gay territory. Somebody texted him, pretending to be me. I think they've cloned my cell phone number. Weird shit's been going on for a few days now."

"Why didn't you tell me?"

"Today's the first time it's gotten serious. Two days ago he came to the house. Kinda embarrassin' with your dad there an' all. He claimed I texted him. He showed it to me. Now unless parts of me are awake and doin' stuff I know nothin' about when I'm sleepin' then all I can say is somebody's fuckin' with us, and I don't know why."

"You think it's Cledus?"

He shook his head. "Nah. It's not his style. He's more the kick the shit out of me first then ask questions later type."

That was true. I didn't know what to say. We obviously had problems in our ranks. Maybe somebody wanted Jerry out of the club. Maybe it had nothing to do with our crew. What the hell had he got himself into? Who had he pissed off?

My cell phone rang. A text. A private number. I looked at the readout. I couldn't believe my eyes.

You're next.

Holy shit. I showed my text readout to Calvin, who gaped at it.

My cell rang a second time. Another text. Sue Ellen was arriving on an eight p.m. flight via JetBlue. I hoped to have good news for her by then.

We'd been ambushed, but I didn't know why. Somebody didn't like us, but why? I needed to talk to my father for more reasons than one. Maybe he had some idea of what the hell was going on.

Calvin's cell phone rang, and he pulled a face. He showed me the readout.

Die, fag. Die.

After all my careful strategizing, somebody had figured out we were all gay. Being gay and being in a gang didn't mix. I'd always known that, but the gang was all I knew.

We walked back to the waiting room where one of the emergency room doctors approached us about an hour later. We crowded around him. His nervous gaze shifted from right to left, and he cleared his throat.

"The patient underwent surgery, and he is listed in a grave, but stable condition. He's very lucky that the stab wound, though deep, missed several vital organs, but he had a smaller, more shallow stab wound to the ribs, one of which splintered, entering his bloodstream, complicating things a little.

"He's in recovery right now. I've just been on the phone with his mother, and she has asked that I release no more information at this time. She thanks you all for being here."

A few of the guys began throwing out questions, but he held up his hand. "Sorry. Unless his next of kin chooses to share more, that's all I can tell you." He walked away again.

Calvin sighed and drew me aside. "Who knew you and Jerry were coming out ahead of the others?"

I shrugged. "Everyone did. They all knew he was driving his Corvette here and that we were gonna pick up our bikes. He said he wanted a little time with Teresa. That suited me. I went to the hotel, took a shower, and relaxed."

"And got laid?"

I paused. No need to tell him about Diego. He had nothing to do with any of this, I was certain. Nobody outside the immediate circle had any knowledge of our travel plans. I'd scouted the hotel myself two weeks ago. I'd left it to Jerry to pick which of the three I'd found that he preferred.

"We'll regroup back at the hotel right after you pick up Sue Ellen. Bring her here to see her son. We'll have an honor guard here to protect him. Got a couple of sharp prospects on their way from New Orleans."

"Which ones?"

"Stag and March."

I nodded. I approved of both. Stag was a rare guy in my book. He was an animal rescuer, particularly of injured game. He lived in the wilds near the bayou, rescuing alligators and such. His real love was deer. Louisiana's white-tail deer were his sweethearts. He had a huge property full of them. He guarded them with his life. He wanted to be a gang member because his other love was bikes. As tender as he could be with a bleeding critter's foot, he was lethal with humans who got them that way.

"I have to pick up Sue Ellen in a couple of hours," I told Calvin. "Any idea what Jerry did with the Corvette?"

"None. Where's your bike?"

"No idea. I assumed he'd have it parked on Sixth."

"His bike is still there, and you've got the keys."

"I can't pick up his mom on a hog."

He arched a brow in my direction. "No. S'pose not."

I felt a tap on my shoulder. I turned to find Diego smiling at me.

"I know where the Corvette is. You got the key for it?"

"How the hell do you know where the car is?" I was incredulous and fearful of some kind of plot. It was so obvious Teresa had a hand in all this drama, especially since she hadn't showed up here. I didn't like my chances of getting my hog back in one piece since Jerry had taken it to her place. I wondered what kind of shape his spider ride was in right now.

"Let's just say I recognized it." He flicked a glance at Calvin. "I was walking up to Sixth Street, and it was parked near Fourth."

I realized he must have seen it after leaving me at the hotel, only he didn't want to say so in front of Calvin.

"Want me to take you there?" he asked. "We'll be right back. We can keep a better eye on it here."

"Do it," Calvin said. He jabbed a finger toward Diego. "You drive the 'vette back. Colby, swing by and get his hog—if it's still in one piece."

"Got it." I didn't mind Calvin giving me direction. He was a senior member, and I trusted him, even if his cock was doing the Macarena with someone else other than my dad.

"I know you think I cheated on Cledus, but in case nobody told you, he and Jerry used to fool around plenty."

Geez, Louise. Jerry had done the funky chicken with both my father and Calvin? And me? Couldn't my life ever be normal?

Calvin blew out a sigh. "I'll call yer dad and let him know what's what."

"Thanks." It hadn't occurred to me to call. Better that Calvin did it anyway. I walked outside, wishing Jerry had trusted me enough to tell me what was going on with him and Calvin. Maybe he'd worried that I'd take offense because of my father. I wouldn't have, not really—not if he could have explained. Was he in love with Calvin? There were more than twenty years between them, but Calvin had a youthful spirit. I'd always been convinced my father had been born grouchy and old.

If Jerry had told me about the strange phone calls and about him and Calvin, I wouldn't have been blindsided by all of this. I took a deep breath and followed Diego outside. I had no idea why I was willing to trust the man, but I was. I also knew Jerry wouldn't have wanted anyone else retrieving his car or his precious spider bike.

Diego handed me a helmet, and I took it, strapping it to my head. It surprised me to look up and see that dusk was approaching. Stars already poked at the sky's darkening canopy. We'd lost several hours and all track of time inside the hospital.

"Thanks for everything," I said, feeling and sounding inadequate as I climbed behind him on the bike.

"No problem." Just as he was about to kick start the engine, my cell phone rang. Diego paused, looking over his shoulder at me. I withdrew the phone from my jacket pocket and checked the readout. Calvin. I took the call, switching it on loudspeaker so I didn't have to take off the helmet again.

"Take a swing by Teresa's house. I wanna know if she's home," Calvin said and ended the call.

"We should go on my bike," Diego said. "You'll be too conspicuous on that fancy thing your friend owns—not to mention the Corvette."

He was right. "Thanks again." I leaned back.

"Where does she live?"

Geez, I was really losing the plot today. "I know how to get there by sight. Can't really give you directions. You okay with me shouting as we go along?"

"No problem," he said again and fired up his hog. He was a smooth, confident rider. I'd known that the first moment I'd spotted him on his way to Austin. He drove like he fucked, like he wanted every second to last.

I'd never been to the hospital before but soon figured out where I was. I gave him directions until we hit Martin Luther King Boulevard.

"About five miles now," I yelled.

He gave me a thumbs up.

I kept my arms around his waist. He felt good. I tried not to think about that. We were on a mission.

"When you see Canoga Avenue, make a left," I called out. He nodded.

It didn't take us long to reach her property. It was as neat, yet nondescript, as I remembered it. A long, low building in front. Rows and rows of produce in back. There didn't seem to be anyone there. No vehicles. No lights inside.

"Want to look around?" he asked, stopping right out front.

There were no vehicles close by—certainly no bikes. I had no idea where the hell mine was. And I loved that hog, too.

Across the road was a feed store that was closed, and again, no vehicles lurked near it.

"Keep going," I said.

He did—all the way past the next several properties. I shouted for him to turn around again. He did. The desolation was eerie. This time, I asked him to ride out back of Teresa's place. Not sure what I expected, but I sure did expect to see some bikes around the joint. Jerry was a collector and owned about fifteen vintage pieces he'd brought out here. None of them were in evidence, and the small barn we rode up to seemed filled with canning equipment.

I had the eerie feeling we were being watched, and apparently so did Diego.

"The flatlands have eyes," he joked.

Man, did I want to tangle with him again.

He looked over his shoulder at me. "Ever fucked in a bale of hay?"

"No, sir." I grinned at him. Could we be this stupid? "Not here. I'd be interested in, ah, maybe taking a rain check on the hay sometime."

He grinned back. "I'll keep it in mind."

We roared back to town, past where he'd seen the Corvette. It was no longer there. On Sixth Street, when we were able to get past the constant stream of new arrivals, the colliding music was louder than ever, and the bar we'd been in seemed to be back in action. We rode past where the spider hog had been. It, too, was gone.

Damn it.

I called Calvin, who didn't seem surprised by anything I had to tell him. "Don't go in there," he warned when I mentioned the bar being back in full swing. "I smell a trap. A big one. They want us looking for revenge. We just won't give it to 'em . . . yet."

He urged me to ride around a bit and see if maybe some spider fans had moved the bike farther up Sixth or even around the corner. We hunted along the streets when, suddenly, Diego gave a yell and began to speed up.

Damn! Some asshole was riding the spider bike. He disappeared along Congress, and we lost him once he realized we were on his tail. We pulled over, and once again I called Calvin.

"Somebody's playing cat and mouse," he said. "Don't follow him. I can't risk losing you and Jerry."

"Is he all right?" I asked. "Any news?"

"None, yet. But that's good news, medically speaking. "

He was right about the cat and mouse angle. The guy on the spider rode right by us.

"You'd better rent a car to collect Sue Ellen," he said. "Pick her up and bring her right back here. Stag and March'll be here in a few hours. I want everyone together until then." Once again, he ended our call.

I put the helmet back on.

"Artificial moonlight," Diego suddenly said. He was looking straight ahead, so I wasn't sure I'd heard what I thought I did.

"Say what?"

"Artificial moonlight," he said, turning to look at me. "It's when you feel safe under cover of darkness, but you're really not. I don't think you should go back to your hotel tonight. I know some place we can go."

I had no words for what he'd just told me. I'd never felt safe at night growing up because that was when Cledus was at his worst. The concept of romantic moonlight to me was the artifice. But I kinda got what Diego was saying.

We drove out toward the airport, no sign of the spider bike. I was surprised when he pulled off to a residential street. We stopped. As early as it was, the place seemed to be sleeping. And then I got it. The houses were all empty. I saw the For Sale signs and realized it was a new development.

He parked at the end of the cul-de-sac between two homes. He turned off the engine and turned to me. "This is the only furnished house. It's quite comfortable, and we're safe here."

"How do you know?" I asked, as we got off the bike and walked to the back door.

"A friend asked me to come look it over for him. The realtor showed me around. I kept a close eye on the lockbox when he brought me here a couple of weeks ago. Unless he changed the combination, we can easily get in."

At the back of the house, he switched on a pocket flash-light dangling from his keychain. He put it between his lips as he wrestled with a lockbox attached to the handle of a sliding glass door. He pressed numbers into the keypad as I watched. I kept staring at his mouth. I'd never been so jealous of an inanimate object before.

As soon as the keypad popped open and he retrieved the house key, he grabbed the flashlight again.

"What's it like inside?" I asked, peering into the darkened house.

He grinned. "It's nice, but not my style at all."

"What is your style?"

"This." He unlocked the sliding glass doors and pushed me inside. I could smell a rosemary plant strongly and wondered where it was. Diego laughed as he pushed me over to a long, leather sofa and got on top of me. We danced with our tongues, our hands and feet tangling as we fought to remove our trousers, shoving them down to our feet. His hair felt silky in my hands as I held it between my fingers.

He slipped down my body, shoving down my underpants to grasp my cock with his open lips.

I couldn't take it. His warm, wet mouth was too much.

"Me, too," I gasped, so he flipped around on top of me. I slid down his black boxer briefs to retrieve his cock. I moaned as he sucked in my length and I began sucking him in a feverish way. He tasted so good.

There was nothing but our sounds and the small shaft of light from the pocket flashlight that had fallen on the floor.

I squeezed his tight ass as his balls bounced on my face. Big and juicy, they beckoned me, but I didn't want to release his mighty cock. I fondled his balls and felt around his ass-cheeks for his crack. His ass tightened, and I gleaned a few drops of pre-come against my tongue.

We came together, his hips banging against my head. I

held him still. Well, as much as I could. He came hard, and so did I.

When we finally stopped pushing and pulling against one another, I relaxed my hold on his shaft, and he slid out of my mouth. I swallowed his load. Very tasty. I couldn't remember the last time I'd wanted someone so badly. So badly, I was breaking my own one-time-only rule.

"Fuck," I whispered, as he worked his way off me. His feet hit the floor, and he lay back against my chest. My orgasm was still ripping through me. It had been a fast and dirty thrill, going at each other like this. We fell asleep like that, and when he stirred some time later, I wanted the world to stop. Once again, it didn't.

"We should go," he murmured against my temple. "Not that I want to."

"Neither do I."

"I wanted this time alone with you, Colby." He turned and looked at me then. There was nothing artificial about the moonlight falling on his sharp, handsome features. God, he was handsome.

Diego reached down and stroked back a few strands of hair from my face.

"What caused you such pain?" he suddenly asked. "I feel it each time I'm near you."

He took me by surprise. The smell of rosemary hit me as I took a deep breath.

Rosemary signified remembrance.

Garnet Beauty. She was my pain. I'd never been able to tolerate cruelty — not to children, animals, or the elderly. And I was certain my beautiful sister had endured unspeakable agony.

"I'll tell you some time," I said, unable to keep my gaze on his gorgeous face. I had no idea why I'd even confessed that much, but he'd gotten me at a vulnerable moment.

"We should go," he said again and rose from the sofa. His cock was half-hard, making it difficult for him to dress. I laughed as I got up too and had just as much trouble getting my jeans back up my legs.

Locking up again, we walked back down the side of the house and got back on his bike.

We roared up the street, the wind whipping our faces as if to punish us for our illicit interlude.

He dropped me at the entrance to the airport car rental section. Letting the bike idle between his thighs, he grinned at me.

"I'm gonna head back to the hospital. By the time you get there, though, we'll be gone."

"I wanna thank you and your crew again for helping us out today. I owe you, big time."

His grin widened. "Yeah, you do."

"Where are you gonna go?" I asked.

"I haven't decided yet. But I've lost my appetite for the bike rally."

"Me, too." I paused. "Can I have your number?"

His mouth twitched, and I caught a gleam of what was it . . . mischief in his gaze?

"I'll find you," he said and took off with a roar as I handed back his spare helmet. My gut ached, and I chided myself. I wasn't developing feelings for this man. No, siree. I wasn't.

Inside the terminal, I marched over to the first available counter, which was Thrifty car rentals and opted for a mid-size car. The attendant gave me the envelope and keys, then told me where I'd find the vehicle. He explained the many toll roads in Austin and that if I used any, the vehicle was registered with the state's EZ-Pass system and I'd be billed to my credit card if I used them.

I made a mental note to avoid them if I could. I thanked him and ran across the terminal to the JetBlue arrivals gate and checked for Sue Ellen's flight. Her plane was about to land.

Waiting by the baggage claim area, I wasn't sure if she'd checked luggage, but I saw her coming down the escalator. She threw herself in my arms. Sue Ellen must have been a beauty in her day. She is still pretty. A very pretty woman, but there are moments when I see the bombshell I knew she'd been as a girl. She was a trip. Her dark hair was cut to the shoulders and dead straight, though I knew it was naturally curly. She looked thirty but was on the other side of fifty. Reed-slim and tough-looking, she'd been a burlesque dancer in her youth—in New York, of all places. She'd married Peter—who went by Punch—McGraw, a Staten Island Coast Guard of all things and he'd loved her raucous ways until his straight-laced parents came to visit them shortly after their marriage thirty-three years ago.

I'll never forget the first time I had dinner with her and Jerry. She'd made teriyaki chicken, the most exotic thing I'd ever eaten in my life, and she told me about her past. I'd loved her instantly when she described dancing with nothing but a tiny pair of panties and high heels. The waiters in her club would suddenly yell "Ice, ice!" which was how the dancers knew the police were in the house and the girls would all put pasties on their nipples.

Jerry had heard the stories before and kept saying, "Aw, Ma," but he seemed to take it in stride. I was fifteen and smitten with her. She was the bomb. She told me how she'd taken the weekend off work when her new in-laws arrived in Manhattan, eager to meet her. She and Punch had gone to JFK Airport to pick them up, and they'd taken a bus into the city. They'd walked around the posh Fifth Avenue stores, and she'd said how well they seemed to be getting along. Then they walked too far and wound up in the wrong neighborhood. There on the side of a building was a gigantic, eleven-foot long poster of Sue Ellen, wearing her panties, pasties, and red high heels.

"His mama never got over it," Sue Ellen told me. "But his father thought I was wonderful!"

She gave up her career and her coast guard when he started staying out late, screwing around on her. She went back to her home in Louisiana to raise her baby, Jerry. Punch soon followed her and more or less stayed in line as far as other women went, but he played pretty hard with his Death Proof buddies.

Punch died two years ago. Alcohol poisoning. By then Sue Ellen had become his caretaker, and the love had long ago died. She had put everything into Jerry, and now she was in real danger of losing him, too.

I'd never seen her vulnerable before, and it felt good, and right, that I could hold her and offer her comfort. For a long moment, she stood in my arms, and I could smell the scent of Jean Nate on her skin. She seemed so thin and frightened; I wrapped my arms more tightly around her. Sue Ellen tucked her head under my chin.

"Okay," she said, pushing herself away from me, tears glittering in her eyes. "Tell me what happened."

As we walked to the car, I told her what I knew. I told her about the bar brawl but had reached the point where I wasn't sure if I should tell her about Jerry's involvement with Calvin when she asked, "Why would somebody want to hurt Jerry? You think it could be Cledus?"

"Cledus?" That shocked me.

"I know Jerry's been fool enough to get involved with Calvin." Before I could protest, she held up a manicured hand. "Hear me out for a moment. I've had some time to think about this. He's had this father fixation a long time, and Calvin's been sniffin' around my boy for years."

"He has?"

She nodded. "I thought maybe your pa found out, but they've been discreet. No. I think Teresa found out, but somebody must have told her. She's been sore at Jerry ever since he told her he wasn't gonna bail out her tomato farm."

"Her farm's in trouble?"

She nodded. "He paid off her property taxes she's owed for a few years and was on the verge of losing it. She wanted more, though." She paused. "She wanted to get into hydroponics, if you get my drift."

I looked around me. I got her drift. I knew Jerry smoked and liked grass a lot, but had no idea developing a business had even been a subject for discussion.

"She has a couple of grows. Clandestine ones. Jerry told me all about it." She gave me a curious look. "You mean, he never told you about it?"

I shook my head. I had no idea.

We found the car and got in. It had three-quarters of a tank of gas, but the paperwork said it should be full. Did I want to hassle with fighting over a quarter of a tank? No, I did not.

I reversed out of the parking space, certain I could smell gas.

Sue Ellen started to sniff. She could, too.

A car came behind us.

Shit. I saw the guns and pushed her down before the first shot was fired. I smacked into the car behind us, ignoring the sickening sound of metal on metal and drove off, with bullets pinging off the car.

The brakes weren't working, but I didn't care. We had to get out of there.

I heard the sound of honking as people rushed from all over the place to watch us.

Shocked to see Diego and another guy on bikes, Sue Ellen and I got out of the car and let it careen into a wall as she and I jumped onto the backs of the bikes, Sue Ellen clutching Diego's hips.

We outran the car shooting at us. I gritted my teeth the whole way to the hospital, shaky as hell when we reached the entrance.

Diego turned and looked at me, as Sue Ellen got off the bike. She was one cool lady. "You need to get your friends and get the hell out of town," he said. "Somebody's put a bounty on your hide, Colby. You're no longer death proof."

CHAPTER FIVE

Diego

I'd hung around longer than I'd intended. I really wanted to blow this place big time. I hadn't ridden all the way out to Austin to get into the middle of some biker war. Nor did I enjoy dodging bullets the way that we had. After that little tango in the bar where Colby's buddy got stabbed, my mind was spinning. And then the gunfire . . . This night had been one surprise after another, and frankly, I'd had enough surprises. So, I'd dropped off Sue Ellen and said goodbye to Colby. I needed to be alone. I needed to think. I went for a drink and did what I do best, listen. I'd never been a big talker. I said what I needed to say and that was it. Listening was something most people didn't do enough of, and that's why they never knew what was going on. I always listened.

I hadn't known who Colby was when I went to his hotel. I really hadn't cared much. He was hot, and he was willing. That was all I needed to know at that time, but now things had changed.

I never assume too much too fast because appearances can be deceiving. Initially, I put him down for a rich kid looking for a thrill cut from the dangerous side. I never went past that. Then in that bar earlier, I found out the guy was a member of Death Proof and the son of Cledus Young. Colby didn't seem like the biker type at all, even if his father had been a badass. But, as I say, assuming is for idiots.

Death Proof was once a gang to be reckoned with in the

bad old days when Cledus Young ran the pack. Now, Cledus was considered a respectable businessman, and Death Proof consisted of a band of petty criminals led by a guy obsessed with bugs . . . spiders, of all things—hence, his nickname.

The Banni had been known to recruit members of lesser gangs occasionally, but mostly we didn't mix with other gangs. Our rival and main competition was the Texas Crushers. We'd had some bloody times with those guys. We were pretty evenly matched but the TC leader, nicknamed Badger, was a guy always looking for shit. And usually, those types found it pretty fast.

The sun was on the verge of rising in the sky when I got back to the campground. Two days had passed, but it felt like a year. So much had happened. Everyone was asleep. I wasn't surprised to see that Chase wasn't around. I was always having to hunt him down. I found a bench to sit on and pulled out my cell phone.

Chase wasn't going to like this, but I didn't give a shit. Chase and I respected each other's boundaries. We often disagreed. I knew he was afraid I'd challenge him for leadership one day because he'd seen me fight. He didn't ever want to be on the receiving end of my fist. But I never wanted to be leader. He had nothing to fear in that respect.

I listened as the phone rang several times.

"Hello," a female voice answered, soft and sleepy.

"Put Chase on the phone," I said.

"Hey, baby. What's your name?"

"Haven't you had enough cock yet?"

There was silence. Then I heard her voice bellow. "Chase. Some asshole!"

I smiled and waited. I'd been called worse.

A few minutes later, Chase said, "This better be good."

"Come back to bed, baby boy," Another female voice

cooed in the background.

Baby boy? Jesus Christ. "I got into a bar fight last night."

"So? What do you want, a medal? You kill somebody?"

"No. I defended a member of Death Proof."

"Death Proof? I didn't think there were any of them guys out here for the rally."

"A few. And it looks like they're on somebody's wipeout list."

"So, send 'em a wreath."

"I think the Texas Crushers may be behind it. Looks like they recruited a bunch of Aussies as foot soldiers to start the party."

"Aussies?"

"Yeah, from Australia?"

"Don't be a smartass. I know you been to college and all, but I do know where those fucking kiwis hail from."

"Ah . . . kiwis are New Zealanders. Anyway, these Aussies are all the way from LA. They're a subchapter now of the Texas Crushers."

"When in fuck did that happen?"

"After the gangland killings in California two years back."

"Oh, yeah. Right. I thought the Aussies were all killed off."

"Apparently they've been resurrected."

"You been a busy boy, D. Hope you took time to get laid during your adventures."

"Your concern for my sexual activity, or lack thereof, is touching, Chase, but we got a big grow-op concern here, courtesy of Spider McGraw's ex. She went ballistic on him in the bar and just about killed him for stepping out on her."

"How Days of our Lives. Why should I care if some spider wants to bedhop?"

"She might be in over her head, trying to play with some

pretty dangerous characters, including the TC. From the looks of it, I think she accidently set up a gang war over some weed."

"Are we talking a major shitload?"

"I doubt the Texas Crushers would bother trying to wipe out Death Proof over a few plants."

"What about Badger? Was he there?"

"None of the Crushers were there, just their errand boys."

"Um. Okay, find this weed."

"What?"

"Find the weed, man."

"No."

"What do you mean *no*?"

"I'm splitting. I've had it. You check it out. I have just one recommendation. If you take Death Proof under our protection, the Crushers will back off, giving us time to find out if this grow-op is worth it. We can make some members of Death Proof the guardians. I'm sure Spider will make up with his old lady eventually."

There was silence.

"You there or is your mouth full?"

"Make it happen."

"Fuck, man." I sighed.

"Take Nuts with you."

"Isn't he with you?"

"No. He went back to the campground a few hours ago."

"Nuts can do —"

"You, Diego. I want you to do it. There'll be no fucking around. What in hell's your hurry to get out of here anyway? You knock up some broad or something? Afraid some kid in ten years will show up on your door and call you Daddy?" He chuckled.

I sighed. "No man, that's your story, not mine."

"Fuck you, man."

I sniggered.

"Give Death Proof our full protection. Let it be known anyone touches them, it will be like touching one of us. We can keep 'em at the clubhouse back home until we know it's safe. How many are we talking about?"

I was beginning to wish I'd kept my mouth shut. "Three or four, I'm not sure, but why not send a couple of members to their pool hall and—"

"Call me back when things are on track." He hung up.

I groaned. I almost threw my phone into the bushes, I was so pissed. I got off the bench and followed the sound of snoring. I reached in and grabbed Nuts by the ankles and dragged him out of the tent. He was mad as a bull. "What the fuck . . . Champagne, I'm going to skin you like a gator and throw you into a boiling hot pot of jambalaya, you fuck!"

He was spitting and snorting, which woke the others up. I leaned against a tree and watched him. He was frothing at the mouth. Not a pretty sight, that huge round belly covered with drool and his huge underpants hanging off his fat ass. Maudit, it was enough to put me off men all together. "It's after eight o'clock." I checked my watch. "Birds are tweeting."

"Parade doesn't start until two, you son of . . . fucking . . . Creole, Cajun whore, whore master, fuck head, son of a . . . And I'll tweet you with those birds!"

I put out my hand as he tried to struggle to his feet. He fell twice, trying to slap it away.

Dave, Arnie, Marcel, and Camden all crawled out of the sack to see what was happening. They were all laughing. Nuts turned his wrath on them. I just smirked as Nuts crawled over to Dave and swung at him. Dave just swayed out of the way.

"When you're finished punching the air," I said, "we need

to talk."

He glared at me, pointing his finger. "You're fuckin' lucky. Must be your birthday, boy!"

I smiled. "Marcel, the canteen is open. Get us some coffee." I handed him a bill.

"I'm on it." He saluted me and raced off, the others all barking other things at him.

"Go put something on," I told Nuts. "We'll talk when I can stand the sight of you."

He gave me the finger and crawled back in the tent, sputtering away.

"This better be big, man," Dave said.

They were all looking at me with expectation.

"Arnie, call one of the hang arounds and tell them to make sure there will be beds at the clubhouse for at least two guys, maybe more."

"Who we bringing back?" Camden asked.

"Some Death Proof members."

They all stared at me.

"Wait until Nuts gets out here. I'll give you the lowdown. Then Nuts and I need to be somewhere."

Nuts came out dressed now, with a half-scowl, half-smile on his face. He glared at me. "Okay, good thing I love you, or you'd be six feet under just about now. What in fuck has got your skinny little ass on fire, boy?"

"Was in a fight with some Aussies last night."

He sobered. "TC henchmen."

"You got it. They attacked the leader of Death Proof."

"Spider McGraw? Why?" Nuts lifted an eyebrow. "The guy is harmless."

"His girlfriend tried to kick the shit out of him, but she wasn't alone. I think she was backed by TC's boys over a grow-op."

"Big one?" Dave asked.

"I don't know. I need to find out. We also need to take these guys under our wing, or they're all dead. Chase says they're officially under our protection. They need to be taken back to the clubhouse until things die down."

"Done," Nuts said. "How do we find them?"

"Come with me," I said. "The rest of you pack up. We'll be leaving soon. Be ready. Wait for my call. Camden, get in touch with the others. Tell them to start heading in our direction, and we'll meet up. We may need more show of strength if the TC gets wind of this."

Camden walked away with his phone in hand.

Marcel came back with a tray filled with coffee. Nuts and I grabbed ours and kept going. Nuts tossed two packs of sugar in his, and I took mine black. A few minutes later, we were on our hogs and ready to ride.

I wanted to keep on rolling, the sun on my face, and the wind in my hair. It wasn't going to happen. I hoped to hell Colby wasn't going to give me a hard time about this. What did they say? Don't shoot the messenger.

When I pulled up in front of the swanky hotel, Nuts looked surprised. "What's here?"

"Colby Young," I told him. "Even though I told him not to, I'm sure he's here."

"How'd you know?" he asked, feeling his pockets. "Hell, no nuts."

"We'll get some later." *He's forgotten the first question. Good.*

As soon as we walked into the lobby, a man behind the counter scurried over. We weren't exactly standard fare, and we both wore our colors.

"May I help you, gentlemen? Do you have a reservation?"

"No," Nuts said. "Do you have any nuts?"

The man blinked.

"He means peanuts," I said. "Don't worry. I'm here to see someone. Can you call Colby Young?"

72

"And you are?" He wasn't the same guy I'd seen before, but he was just as snotty.

"Diego. Tell him Diego is here. It's very important that I see him."

"Wait here." The man marched off. Nuts began to imitate the man's walk, bobbing up and down like a peacock.

"Stop," I told him. We were attracting attention.

The man in the blue suit suddenly motioned to me. "And who is the . . . person with you?" He asked, giving Nuts the once over and then wrinkling his nose.

"Tell Mr. Young it's a friend of mine, and we need to see him."

The man returned to the phone, spoke a minute, then waved his hand toward the elevator.

Nuts followed me, and we waited for the elevator to come down. Nuts was sniggering all the way up and imitating that walk again. I rolled my eyes. When the door opened, Nuts stopped bopping around and seemed in awe. He became spellbound by all the mirrors and such. "Holy shit," he muttered. "I'm in the wrong club."

Directly ahead of us was the older guy I'd seen at the hospital the night before. He was shirtless and lounging on the sofa, drinking something out of a fancy cup. Calvin. That was his name. He waved at us. "Colby is in the bedroom."

When we walked into the living room, Colby glanced first at me, then at Nuts. Then his gaze went back to me and stayed there. He sat up straight then rose from the sofa, back to the door, as if to block our entry.

"What . . . what are you guys doing here?"

Colby had come out of the bedroom. He was wearing only a pair of jeans, and his hair was still wet. This was interesting. What had they been up to?

"What's going on?" Colby asked again.

"Didn't the front desk call you?" I asked.

"Yeah." He narrowed his eyes and came to stand beside Calvin. "Still doesn't explain what you're doing here."

My gaze settled on Calvin. They seemed pretty chummy. Obviously, the guy had spent the night. And if my gaydar was operating correctly, Calvin was not straight. He was trying hard not to check me out, but he was losing the battle.

"Want to thank you for last night, man—what you did," Calvin said.

Colby was eyeing Nuts.

"You're officially under the protection of the Banni," I said. "We're going to escort you home, and until we're sure what's going on, you'll stay at our clubhouse."

Colby's eyes widened. "What did you say?"

"You heard me." I looked around. "Get your shit. I need to know who else we have to pick up."

"We're not picking up anyone." Colby shook his head. "If this is over the shooting, that was just a threat. Spider claims he knows who's behind it and—"

"Listen, that was no threat. It was real." I met his gaze. "The TC wants to eliminate Death Proof. Those Aussies were working for the TC. The TC is our main rival. Therefore, we protect you."

He scowled. "What the hell for?"

Calvin was glancing down at his hands.

I moved a little closer. "Why don't we ask your friend here?"

"Calvin?" Colby demanded. "Why in hell would the TC want to kill us off? We're not their competition."

Calvin looked up. "We were going to tell you. We were going to tell everyone, then well . . . Spider and I . . . you know. Teresa was pissed and . . . you know the tomato farming wasn't going so well."

Nuts looked at me and mouthed "tomato farm."

"Spider's old lady . . . well . . . she didn't know about us, and I was going to stop. I was going to go back to your father and beg on my hands and knees. I—"

"You guys all... ah... are into each other?" Nuts blurted.

"Nuts," I sighed. "Go wait in the lobby. I'll be there soon."

He shook his head and walked to the door.

"Okay," I said after Nuts left, "enough of this. You guys can argue later about all this touchy-feely shit. Colby, how many members are here at the rally?"

"Just me, Calvin, and Spider."

"Okay, the ones back home?"

"They'll be all right; they're just prospects."

I looked at Calvin. "Tell me the truth. How many plants?"

Colby stared at me. "What are you—"

"Thousands," Calvin said. "All underground, so they can't be detected. The tomato crops in the fields are a decoy."

"This just didn't happen overnight. This has been in the works for a while. Takes time to build all that underground. You make any deals with the TC yet?"

"No."

"What about Spider's old lady?"

"We don't know. She won't talk to me. She's cut us off."

"We gotta go find her or she won't be talking to anyone."

"Wait." Colby put a hand on my forearm. "Do what you want. I want no part of this."

"You're coming with me," I told him.

"Fuck you." Colby shook his head. "I'm not going to be your prisoner."

Colby turned around and walked toward the bedroom. It was then I saw something like a flash in the window. It didn't seem right at all. "Colby!" I yelled, and then I leaped like a freaking ballet dancer in The Nutcracker and fell right on top of him. I glanced at Calvin, who was on the floor by the sofa. "Stay down!"

A rain of gunfire riddled the windows seconds later, and I put my arms over Colby's head and pressed him to the carpet.

The gunfire stopped abruptly, leaving a blur of smoke and the smell of sulfur in the air. My cell phone rang. "Fuck!" I didn't like being shot at.

Colby pushed me off him and got to his feet. I stood and opened my phone.

"What the fuck happened up there? You in one piece, Diego?" It was Nuts.

"Yeah," I said, glancing at Calvin and Colby, who were hugging each other. "Everyone's fine. We're being watched. Call the guys. Get them to patrol the outside of the hotel. I want to make sure no one's around before we take these guys out of here. I want them taken back to the campgrounds and kept there until I see Madame Pot Farmer and Spider Boy."

"I hear you."

I hung up.

"Get dressed," I said to Calvin and Colby. "Be ready. We stay here and stay low until I think it's safe to leave."

"The police will be here soon," Calvin said. "I'm sure they've been called." He was shaking. "What do we say to them?"

"Nothing. We'll be out of here by the time they arrive."

"What about those guys who shot at us?" Calvin asked.

"The sound of the sirens and the bikes will drive the TC away. They won't risk another assault now." I moved slowly over to the bullet-ridden windows, stood to the side, and kept watch.

"I'm going to get dressed," Calvin said.

I glanced at him. "Remember, stay away from the

windows."

"I hear you."

"You saved my life again," Colby said suddenly. "This is getting to be a habit. You must like me."

I looked over at him. "I'm just following orders. That's all."

"You don't seem the type to follow orders. Just what does it take to master you?"

I gave him a faint smile.

"Why aren't you the leader of the Banni?"

"Because I don't want to be."

"That's what I thought," he said.

"You do a lot of thinking about me and the Banni, do you?" I glanced out the window again.

"No. It's just interesting to figure out what makes a man like you tick."

I narrowed my eyes. "You never cease to amaze me. Someone just tried to shoot our heads off, and you're wondering what makes me tick."

"I have nothing to do with Teresa's grow."

"I don't care. The TC think you do, so that's it."

"I run a fucking pool hall."

I didn't comment. Colby could plead innocent all he wanted to me—wouldn't change anything. He was lumped in with the others. He was marked. My job was to keep him alive. That's all.

"You think Spider knows all this?"

"He's your leader. What room is he in at the hospital? I need to see him."

"In three-zero-eight but . . . it's not his fault. I think he's lost control of Teresa."

"Because he was fucking Calvin."

"Calvin's my father's lover, you know. Not mine."

"I didn't ask. Don't want to know."

"No, but I saw your face when you saw him on my sofa. You think I fucked him last night."

"I don't think anything. It's not my business."

"You were jealous."

"You'd really like to think so, Mr. Have-a-rule-you-don't-fuck-the-same-guy-twice." I walked away from the window.

"I didn't break my rule," he protested. "Well, maybe um, slightly." His cheeks flamed. He was cute when he got embarrassed.

"Slightly?" I cocked a brow at him.

He glanced away from me. "Okay, so we fucked twice. That's the end of it."

"And if we'd had more time, it would have been—"

"Just those two times." He cut me off. "Fooling around is not the same as fucking. It's foreplay, and guys who look like you are good for foreplay."

"Is that so?"

"Uh-huh. Want to know why?" He reached for a T-shirt he'd left on the chair and put it on.

"No." I shook my head. "Not really."

"I'm going to tell you anyway."

"Somehow I knew that."

He smiled at me. "I'm making nice with you. You're going to get me out of this building and then you're going to fuck off."

I leaned against the wall. That wasn't going to happen.

"Anyway, the reason men like you are . . ." He trailed off as we heard the sirens in the distance.

"Okay." I grinned at him, "Saved by the sirens. Let's go."

Colby gave me a dirty look.

Calvin came running out of the bedroom with a bag. I pressed the elevator button, and when the door opened, we descended to the second floor.

"Hey," Calvin said, "this isn't—"

"We take the stairs." As we walked out, I made a call. "Have the guys meet us in the parking lot at the back of the hotel. Ground floor. Now." I hung up.

Just when it seemed like Colby was about to give me a hard time, I grabbed his arm. Several of the club members came roaring into the parking lot and surrounded us as we stepped outside. "Don't give me grief," I told him, meeting Colby's angry eyes.

Calvin got on the back of Nuts' Harley right away, without trouble.

"Now why can't you be a good boy like your friend there?" I shook my head.

"I don't need your fucking . . . I'll show you a good boy . . . you . . ."

Marcel pulled up in the van. "Put Colby in the back," I said, pushing him toward Dave and Arnie.

"You son of . . ." Colby yelled. "You . . . damn you, Diego! Don't do this to me."

He was struggling, and the other two guys were doing all they could to control him.

I sighed. "Damn it. Do I need this?" I growled and walked over to him. "Give him to me." I motioned with my hand. With one heave, I threw him over my shoulder like he was a sack of potatoes. The van was open in back. I dumped him in on top of a bunch of bags. He let out a howl, but it wasn't of pain, it was pure rage. "I don't need you to . . . I can take care of myself."

I glanced at Marcel in front. "Get out. Leave us a minute."

Marcel hopped out and walked away.

I crawled into the van on top of Colby and let the door close behind me.

"Get off me." He bucked his hips.

I looked down into his face. "Listen to me, Colby," I hissed. "I'm trying to save your damn life." I pressed his wrists to the floor of the van.

He calmed for a minute. I lowered my head, not enough to kiss him but close enough so that he could almost feel my mouth on his. I let the length of my body press against his for a moment—um... just enough pressure to make it pleasurable. I heard nothing but his breathing, which was coming out a little heavily. "What was it you were trying to say about men like me and foreplay?"

"Fuck off," he muttered, but his voice was sober.

"Are we calm now?"

His mouth moved to my ear. "Listen to me. I'll never need you or crave you the way you want me to, Diego. I'll never need any one man to protect me or to fuck me. You're one of many. Just remember that—just one cock among many. I've had your cock now, and I don't need it again."

I lifted my head. He was really pissing me off. "Okay, fine, and you remember this." I grabbed his hand and pressed it against my cock. "Because we both agree, it's the last time you're going to feel it."

I was hard, and so was he.

He tried to pull his hand away, but I held it against me. "And this," I grunted, lowering my mouth to his. He bit my lip as I went to kiss him. I tasted the blood in my mouth, but I kept on, my kiss deepening until he yielded to me and began to return the kisses. I heard the lowest of moans come from him, then I pulled away.

"Now you're calm." I gave him a smug smile. "Before you go giving me speeches, little boy, make damn sure your body will cooperate with your tongue. Seems to me..." I wiped off my mouth with the back of my hand. "They're in conflict."

He kicked out at me and missed.

I laughed and backed out, pushing the door open.

His eyes were sparkling with anger when I took one last

look. If I could have read his mind, I knew he was calling me every nasty name he knew. I smiled at him again then closed both doors. "Take him, Marcel. If he gives you any trouble, tie him up and put a gag in his mouth."

I waited until they'd disappeared from the parking lot then spotted a squad car. Nope. That wouldn't do. I ran around the block then doubled back for my bike. Twenty minutes later, I was on my way.

I got to the hospital, parked my bike, and stripped off my colors. I kept a close eye to make sure no one was following me.

Inside, I took the elevator to the third floor. I got off the elevator carefully and looked around. I headed to room 308 and peeked inside. Spider lay there, blood bag and other fluids hanging overhead. When I walked in, he opened his eyes. "Diego Champagne," he managed.

I don't know how he knew me. We'd never met before. When he saw my confusion, he said, "I saw you fight in Louisiana, underground extreme stuff. Bloody. You're good. Did the guy live to tell the tale?"

"I have no idea." I moved closer. "Why didn't you tell the others?"

"I thought it was a secret. Teresa let the cat out. I think she did it for revenge since I was . . . you know . . ."

"Fucking another guy?"

"You wouldn't understand."

"I'm not your judge."

"Then what do you want?"

"Your woman has somehow let the TC in on this new business of hers. They plan to wipe out your club."

"Oh no." He closed his eyes.

"Chase has put your club under Banni protection."

"Thank the heavens . . ." He looked at me. "Not free."

"Never free."

He shook his head. "Teresa is playing with fire. This is the big time, man. These guys don't negotiate with women. They're playing her. What was she thinking?"

"Love and jealousy do strange things to a person." I paused. "Does Cledus know?"

"About the drugs or about Calvin and me?"

"The drugs."

"Not yet. He's an honorary lifetime member. I'm the leader."

"Do you want us to tell him to watch his ass? They could come for him."

"Please."

"Done. And someone will be coming for you. We have to move you."

He sighed and nodded.

I was ready to go, but he motioned to me. "Don't go yet. There's something I need to tell you."

I came closer. "What's that?"

"You have Colby, right?"

"Yeah, but I can't say it was easy. Guy thinks he doesn't need anyone."

Spider smiled. "That's Colby." Then he sobered. "Something you need to know about Colby and this guy called Franklin. Do you know him?"

"Yeah, he was promoted sergeant at arms for the TC about two years back. Young, blond, big muscular guy, he's a cousin to the leader. What about him?"

"Well, a year ago, Colby and Franklin hooked up in Dallas. They met in a bathhouse, no colors to identify each other. Colby didn't know Franklin was TC. They spent the night in some hotel somewhere. Then Colby sees him in the parade with his colors on last year. Franklin is deep in the closet. He may be on a quest to take Colby. Just be aware. I have a feeling Franklin is scared Colby might out him."

It took me a minute to comment. "Colby gets around, seems to like those sergeants," I said under my breath.

Spider looked at me. "What?"

"Nothing. No worries. Colby will stay with the Banni until it's safe. Where do I find your Amazon woman?"

Spider began to give me directions to the farmhouse.

"I rode out there with Colby. There was nothing there. No bikes, nothing."

"There is another property. End of the block." He closed his eyes. "Colby's never been there." He looked sadder than hell. "I should've told him about the op. I see that now." He told me how to find the second place.

As I was leaving, he said, "Diego?"

I glanced at him.

"Thanks for taking care of Calvin and Colby."

I nodded and left. I made a call to Chase. "Get some men over to the hospital and get Spider out of there now. The TC are going to kill him."

"We're on it."

As I rode to the outskirts of the city, I was thinking about Franklin. What in hell did Colby see in that jackass? Every time I'd met that guy, he'd always say the same thing. "One day, I'm going to face you in a one of those fights, and I'm going to be the one to put you down for good."

"Bring it on," I'd tell him, but he never did.

It started to rain. By the time I got up the muddy road to the farm, I was soaked. All I could see were fields and fields of tomatoes everywhere. That's all I could smell, too.

The house on the second property was small and decrepit, made of planks with peeling paint and solid panes of glass. The place looked as if it was about to fall down.

I walked up onto the porch. It creaked, the wood soft and ready to break through.

I knocked on the door, and the frame rattled. *Jesus.*

"I have a gun," I heard a woman yell.

"I didn't come to harm you, Teresa. I need to speak to you."

"Are you the police?"

"No. You're in a lot of danger, Teresa. I believe I can help you. I'll protect you. Please open the door. You can hold the gun on me if you like." I didn't carry a gun as a practice. Now I wished I had one.

The door opened a little, and a gun barrel poked out. "Okay, slowly, hands up, mister."

I walked in with my hands up. "Hey." I smiled at her. She was a fairly young woman, but she had a face that spoke of hard times. She was thin with strings of dark hair poking through the blonde chunks, and she wore a flowered house dress.

She reached over and patted me some, then smiled. "You're a real handsome bugger."

"Thanks," I said. "Can I put my hands down?"

She shrugged. "I will shoot you if you move."

"I understand that." I looked around the kitchen. Everything was dull and basic. I noticed two mugs with half-drunk tea in them. Chances were, she wasn't alone. "Have the TC been here?"

She nodded. "I'm looking for a buyer. They said not to trust anyone."

"Um. Who else knows about this?"

"Jerry's gang, but they're out now. I want no more to do with him. He was fucking well . . . fucking a guy. You wouldn't understand."

I smiled. "Look, Teresa, the Banni will give you protection in exchange for a deal that would be fair."

"Like what?" She looked suspicious.

"You can't do this alone. You need people to harvest and sell it, move it in big quantities. We can do that and provide the protection you need against rival gangs and looters."

"That's just what they said."

"Tell me what cut they wanted?"

"They said twenty percent for me. Don't you think that's low?"

"That's robbery," I said. "We'd be prepared to be equal partners. We'd do all the work."

"Equal, like fifty-fifty?"

I nodded. It could always be renegotiated.

"Well, I want you to tell that Franklin guy."

I stiffened. "Is he here?"

She nodded. "He's in the cellar."

Fuck. I knew it.

She smiled at me. "He said he'd put his bike round back, figured you'd show up—or at least one of you. He was hoping it was you. Said you were charming but that he once saw you almost rip a man's head off. That true?"

"You had to be there." I stood. "If you want to consider my offer, we'll protect you. You'll be dead if you play with them. I guarantee you."

"Now just what are you telling her, Diego?" A voice said suddenly from behind me. "Not telling stories out of school, are we?"

Teresa smiled at someone behind me. I swallowed. This wasn't good. This wasn't good at all.

CHAPTER SIX

I turned around to look at him. "How nice to see you, Franklin. How've you been?"

"Very well. I see Chase still has you doing his dirty work."

"What are you doing here?" I lifted an eyebrow.

His smile faded. "If you must know . . ." He brightened again, walking over to Teresa. "I've been consoling this poor girl." He smoothed back her hair. "Seems her lover prefers cock to pussy."

"A lot of that going around these days." I met his gaze and smiled.

That was not winning me any favors.

"What do you want, Champagne? Shouldn't you be off beating someone to death?"

"Not for another month."

"Oh."

"I thought you told me one day you'd be there?"

"I will." He looked down at Teresa. "Could you be a dear and leave us for a few minutes, darling. We have some private talk."

She kissed him on the mouth and left the kitchen.

I laughed. "Turning on the charm just for her. How sweet."

"She loves it. Loves cock. Loves my cock."

"I heard you love the bathhouses." I blew him a little kiss.

His expression hardened. "Who told you that?"

I shrugged and met his eyes. "You should watch where

you stick your dick. Malicious gossip, I'm sure."

"Where is he?"

"Where is who?"

"Colby Young?"

"Never heard of him. So, how long does she have?"

He laughed. "You think I'd let her suck my cock, then blow off her pretty head?"

"Frankly, yes," I told him. "But there's no point in killing her. The place doesn't belong to her entirely."

"It will when her beloved dies."

"You see, that's just the thing. I got an email here that says Spider is safe in the arms of . . ."

Franklin hung on my every word. "Jesus? Safe in the arms of Jesus?"

I laughed. "No such luck. The Banni, actually — safe in the arms of the Banni."

His mouth opened. "You fucker."

I shrugged. "Please, Franklin, give me the pleasure of beating you black and blue someday. My pleasures are so few lately."

I saw his hand slide into his pocket. Not good. I lunged for him and grabbed his arm. Damn, I was getting good at this kind of shit. Franklin froze, grunted, and tried to lift his arm. "Leave the gun in there, stud, or I'll break your arm."

He gave me a look that I didn't like so . . . well . . . I broke it anyway.

"You son of a bitch," he yelped.

"Next time, it will be your head." I slid the gun out of his pocket and took out the bullets. I threw the bullets at him and tucked the gun in my belt. "Nice. I'll add it to my collection." I waved and walked back outside. It had stopped raining. That was a good sign.

I was starved. I called Chase from a Greek restaurant where I was pigging out on steak and shrimp.

"It was an ambush. TC's Franklin Kennedy was there, ready to play games. I broke his arm for him." I drank some more wine.

Chase laughed. "That was nice of you."

"He pissed me off. I don't like his face."

"Better reason than none."

"Where are you?"

"TCs wanted a meeting."

"You're not going, are you? We've got Spider. He owns the place."

"Haven't decided. The leader is willing to make some concessions. Seems Spider had some problems with them. It's personal."

"You're negotiating with the TC now? Fuck, Chase!"

"They'll cut us in. No war. Fifty-fifty. No middle man."

"Which means what? You cut Spider out completely? It's his land."

"You don't approve, I see. You get religion?"

"They want our prisoners, too?"

"Only one of them. Colby Young. They don't care about Calvin."

I put down my fork. "No."

"Why not? He's the son of—"

"I know who he's the son of. These fucking personal vendettas are for shit, man!"

"We gain nothing this way, protecting them for what gain?"

"So you'd rather collaborate with the TC, who will stab you in the back, rather than Spider's bunch?" I thought fast. "Don't you want it all? Why split with the TC when we can run the entire thing? Spider's gang is much smaller. We'll swallow them."

"You really want to sell this, man! I want peace. I don't want war, Diego. We've had enough of that, haven't we?

We've lost some good men."

And then it hit me. "That's why you came out here. You knew all this shit."

"I knew some of it. Not all. I didn't make any decisions. We'll have church. It's always a majority vote."

"Fuck, Chase."

"We've got what they want. We won't make a move until I say. For now, we protect these guys. We take it day by day. Happy?"

"Right." I hung up and pushed my plate away. Son of a bitch. Chase could be a double-crossing son of a bitch when he put his mind to it. I got up, paid the bill, and decided to head back to Baton Rouge. It was one-thirty in the afternoon, and if I made good time, I could be back home by ten o'clock or so. I wanted out of this city, to get back home where I belonged.

Every time I leave and come back home again, I'm reminded of history. My history . . . totally wrapped up in this place of hard drinking people obsessed with football. And my blood. Cherise, my mother, always told me I was a true son of Baton.

"I could cut you in quarters, boy. One quarter'd be Spanish, the other French. That's from your daddy's side. And from me, you get one-quarter African and the other English. That's the slave and master side. You're a true mix, boy. Just remember to use the right part for the right act."

She never did tell me which was better for which.

Cherise was the great-great-granddaughter of a beautiful African woman named Abena, who was brought to the shores of the Mississippi on a slave ship in the late 1800s. She was sold to an English steamship magnate named Warren Hemley and worked in his house as a maid. The first son in the family, William Hemley, fell in love with her. Mother said that Abena adored William but despised his father.

When she got pregnant, Hemley sold her to a brutal man. She became a field hand and died a few years later. Her daughter, whose skin was very light, was sold into prostitution and later rescued by another white man named Harold Smith, who freed her and took her as his common-law wife, a practice which was tolerated, especially with mixed-race women. Her name was also Cherise, like my mother, and she was my great-grandmother.

My mother's mother was born free but dirt poor. There was hardly ever enough food to eat and my mother, the eldest, had to fend for herself and her five siblings. My grandfather, also a white man, was killed in a bar fight. I guessed the nut didn't fall far from the tree.

When my mother saw Maurice Champagne, she was dazzled by his good looks and his ability to speak three languages. He was a sharp dresser, had a smooth tongue, and he offered her a way out of poverty. They married and traveled around. My father took on a few extreme fights and was known across the state for being 'one tough bugger.' When he got his big windfall from a fight in New Orleans, he put a down payment on a house.

He could be generous that way, Cherise told me. But when it came to supporting his family and being faithful, he wasn't so tough. Soon after I came along, he was gone.

My mother did what she could—cleaning, cooking, and sewing for others. She took a job as a waitress to try to hold onto the house. As soon as I could walk, I was working, doing gardens, raking leaves, and helping old ladies with their grocery bags.

I hoped I had more of my mother in me, that I wasn't a quitter. But still, I knew the physical strength came from my father. I saw his picture on a poster once. He was fighting somewhere in town. I almost went to see him. I was twelve, and I stood outside the arena staring at that photograph. A stranger, and yet he seemed so familiar. A large, handsome man in his young thirties, well over six feet, with muscular arms and legs. I wanted to go inside and scream at him. *Why? Why did you leave? Don't you know I want to know you?*

I just walked away. I never even told my mother, who I knew never stopped loving him. I'd hear her cry at night sometimes. How could she love that man? He'd deserted her, deserted me. Well, there's no rhyme or reason why people love. They just do.

I slowed down now as I rode through the Baton Rouge Parish, the capital of Louisiana, situated in the southeast-central part of the state on a bluff above the Mississippi River.

You could see it everywhere, its history. It was in the architecture and the restaurants, the music and the accents. The French, the English, and the Spanish had all had their hand in shaping this place. Add to it the flavors of the indigenous tribes of the first peoples and the Africans, forced into slavery by their white masters, who saw them as less than human.

With a history tied to the Mississippi River, Baton Rouge grew from its colonial past as a military outpost into an American city of modern industry and rich diversity. Fire, flood, civil war — they'd seen it all, and Baton Rouge had endured in its traditions and humanity.

It all began when a French explorer had led a party up the Mississippi River and saw a reddish cypress pole festooned with bloody animals and fish; it marked the boundary between the Houma Tribe and the Bayougoula hunting grounds. The French called the landmark tree le bâton rouge, the red stick.

Today, Baton Rouge was one of the largest mid-sized business cities in the United States with its JPMorgan tower and Louisiana state capital. The population explosion was in part due to Katrina, which saw many hurricane victims migrate from New Orleans.

I passed the Tiger Stadium and thought of my mother. It was after ten o'clock, but she'd still be up, huddled in her bathrobe in front of the television in the house I grew up in the southern part of urban Baton, known as the Saint George Parish. It was a mix of affluent whites and native Creole, with an influx of survivors from Hurricane Katrina more recently.

Cherise told me the rich whites now wanted to separate and pay their taxes to 'Saint George,' which would create a ghetto of poor, urban blacks in 'Baton' and rich suburban whites in 'Saint George.'

I was hoping my mom could sell that house and use it for her retirement money. The property value would go way down. I had been urging her to sell now. I'd set her up in a new house, someplace nice. She wouldn't hear of it.

I pulled my bike into the driveway of the little house that my father had put a down payment on over twenty-four years ago. It was still in good shape. Me and the boys had done a lot of work on the roof and the foundation. It was an old house but solid.

Cherise was peering out the window, as were a few of the neighbors. I got off the bike and walked up to the door. My mother answered it, grabbing me by the arm and pulling me inside. My mother was a little bitty thing, standing about five foot two and weighing no more than one hundred and ten. It was funny to see the way she pushed me around.

"Hey, Ma."

"Don't Hey Ma me," she scolded. "Get in here. What's the matter with you, Diego, driving up here on that thing this time of night? And in that jacket, too! I'm catching hell from the busybodies tomorrow, I tell you."

I laughed.

"Oh, you." She slapped me. "Give me a kiss. What's

wrong with you? Forgot your manners?"

I reached down, lifted her off the floor, and gave her a big kiss, along with the bear hug.

She punched me. "Put me down now. Dang it, boy. What's you doing here this time of night? What about that bike thing up in Austin?"

"I came home." I walked into the kitchen. "Did you make cornbread?"

She went to sit in front of the television again. "Help yourself," she said. "Took some over to Nancy's grandmother after I left the scrap. She's been feeling poorly."

I poked in the breadbox and pulled out the cornbread. I sat down with a knife and some butter.

"You using a plate?"

"Ah . . ." I jumped up and got a plate and sat back down, my mouth full. "Yeah."

I heard her laugh.

I stuffed the rest of the buttered cornbread down and put the unused plate in the sink. I walked into the living room and slumped on the sofa. "What'cha watchin'?"

"Some fool show about people running around trying to find things. Imagine making a program outta that." She clicked her tongue.

I smiled, content just to sit there with her like in the old days. Only now she had a fifty-inch high definition flat-screen instead of the old black and white we used have to pound to get straight. I bought this one for her birthday. Damn, she'd made me show her the receipt before she'd take it. "I know them boys you run with. This didn't come from the back of a truck, did it?"

I was chuckling, remembering how stubborn she could be.

She reached over and took my hand. "What's ticklin' you? You have such a nice laugh—your father's laugh. So handsome when he was happy. Not a girl in the parish didn't look twice at him. You look just like him."

I gazed at her, raised her hand and kissed it. "How was work?"

"That why you come back here so fast? Checking on me?"

"No," I said. "That's not why. You do like it, don't you?"

"Salary too damn high for what I do. Don't know what to do with all that money. Leave it in the bank mostly."

"Good." I glanced over at the framed photograph of me on the wall. I was standing on the field, football in my hand. My mother spent one week's groceries getting that picture professionally framed.

"You miss it?" She asked me when I looked down at my hands.

I shook my head and stood. "No. It's over."

"Son," she said, as I walked by her chair, "don't fight no more in those fights like you do. You're gonna get yourself killed."

I smiled at her. "Don't worry about me. I can handle myself."

"There's always someone come along better than you, Diego. One day . . . stop before that day comes."

I leaned down to kiss her cheek. "Gotta go. Thanks for the cornbread. See you at the yard tomorrow."

She grunted. "The scrap, you mean."

I laughed and walked to the door. She always called it 'the scrap.'

"Lock up," I called out before I shut the door.

I waited until I saw her come to the door and wave. I got on my bike and headed to the clubhouse. I needed to check on our guests before I went home. When I got there, I realized I was beat. I pulled my weary bones off my hog and yawned. I doubted I'd make it home.

Marcel's van was parked outside, along with about six

hogs. I cast a glance at the van before walking around to the side door. I was checking for dents in a tongue in cheek way. With the mood Colby had been in when I left him in Austin, I wouldn't have been surprised.

The clubhouse was on Florida Avenue and Greenwell Springs, not far from Merrydale. When I joined the Banni, they had land there, along with a huge warehouse they converted into their club headquarters. When I won a shitload of money from one of my fights, I decided to invest in a custom bike shop. It was my passion. I also spent my time working at the scrap yard. The club owned Banni Scrap jointly. We all profited. It was the biggest one in the parish. The custom bike shop, however, was mine alone.

As I opened the door, I heard music. There was a bit of a party going on. Nothing new there. Chase was home, and that was an excuse for girls and booze. Everything was an excuse for that.

I walked down a narrow hallway into a larger room where there were scattered tables and a fully stocked bar. Several of the members were in house, along with Marcel and Chase.

Two topless girls danced on the bar while Wiley and Free, full-fledged members, leaned on the bar and gawked at the dancers. Some hard rock tune started now, and the girls were really moving, which encouraged some of the others around the bar to clap to the beat and watch the jiggle fest.

On their way to the ladies, they all hugged me, welcoming me back. Chase didn't seem interested in the heavy-breasted duo for once. Instead, he came and sat down at a table with me.

I knew Colby was somewhere here. I tried not to rush right in to see him like some lovesick puppy, although I knew I'd been deliberately putting it off because I wanted to see him. I wanted to do more than that, but it would have to wait. In fact, I'd have to watch it here.

"Wanna beer?" Chase asked, lifting a cold one.

I shook my head. "I'm beat. Gonna pass out."

"Shit."

"What shit?" I eyed him.

"Was gonna ask you to stay with the Death Proof members."

"They giving you grief?" I hid a smile.

"That Colby Young doesn't want our protection. The other one is all right."

"There must be more."

"Cledus told us he's taken care of it."

"So he knows."

"Yeah. He wants us to keep the crazy one and his buddy. I got the feeling he didn't want to see the quiet one . . . Calvin?"

"He called his son crazy?"

"Cledus says he thinks the kid has the insanity gene like his ole' lady. She's in the cracker bin."

I blinked. "Mental institution?"

"That's what I mean, the cracker bin. Anyway, that Colby is unpredictable. We had to tie his hands. He came this close to getting a gag. He shut up just in time. Anyway," Chase sighed, took a sip of his beer, "I'll do it for Cledus. The old man has got the big C. Doesn't have long."

Fuck. A mother in an institution and a father on the way out. Not too lucky. I couldn't help but feel sorry for Colby. But insane? Was Colby insane? No. He was fucked up maybe, like a lot of people, but he didn't seem certifiable.

"I can't stay tonight," I said. "I haven't slept yet."

"Get a few hours. I'll stay until two, then you can take over. I want someone here with Marcel and the other two."

"Okay," I muttered. "I'm going up to see Colby and Calvin then I'll take the back room for a nap. I'll stay tonight.

Where's Nuts?"

"On an errand."

I heard a squeal. One of the girls was on her back, getting mauled. She was about to get more than that, from the looks of it. I walked by and down the hall.

Simon and Herman were on the door, two wannabes always willing to volunteer. They looked scared out of their minds. They stood straight when they saw me. One of them saluted. Hell. "Hey, guys, they in there?"

"The good-looking one is," Herman pushed a pile of red hair out of his eyes. "He got tied up. He was wild, man. The other one, Calvin, is down the hall. Todd is with him. He's cool."

"Okay, unlock the door."

The blond one, called Simon, quickly unlocked it. "You want a cross and some holy water?" He smirked.

I smiled. "No. That's okay. Lock it after me."

"Yes, sir."

I opened the door and walked in, closing it behind me. I heard the lock click. Colby sat in a chair, his legs were tied together, and his hands were behind his back. His head was on his chest. He was dozing.

I came closer. I was glad to see that no one had lost their temper and hit him. He looked fine. I leaned against the wall and folded my arms, watching him.

Colby lifted his head. "What are you grinning at?"

"Still pissed, I see. I thought you would have cooled off by now."

"I'm still here, aren't I?"

I narrowed the distance and pushed some of his hair off his forehead.

"Don't touch me."

I put up my hands. "Okay. Are you thirsty?"

"No. I have to piss."

I glanced at the bathroom door on the other side of the room. "Will you be good if I untie you?"

"Do I have a choice? Do you think I could overpower you?"

"No."

"And even if I could, this place is crawling with you bloodsuckers."

I leaned down and undid the ropes around his legs. Then I reached up and undid one wrist. He pushed my hand away after that and did the rest himself. He jumped up and forged ahead. There was no window in that bathroom and no lock on the door. I let him march in and slam the door in my face. It made him feel powerful.

I waited.

The door opened, and he stood there. "If the TC wants me dead, you won't stop them. You can't keep me here forever."

"Why not?" I watched him walk over to the single bed and sit down.

"Chase will find a reason to get rid of me, hand me over."

"How do you know that?" I narrowed my eyes.

"Then it's true."

I sighed. "He's not sure what to do right now, but we promised your father—"

"My father? What's he got to do with all this?"

"He's connected. It was his club."

"And Spider?"

"He's safe."

"Why go to all this trouble if we're not valuable to you somehow? Do you think I believe you're doing this out of the goodness of your heart?"

"I'm just the messenger."

"You're the enforcer." He met my gaze and held it for a moment.

I looked away.

"I want to sleep. Since I'm locked in here."

I checked the window. It was one solid pane of glass. I saw three wannabes patrolling outside.

"I've already considered that," Colby said, watching me as I looked outside. "Undoable, unless I want my ass shot off."

I smiled at him. "It would be a shame, an ass as nice as yours."

"Fuck off," he told me.

I laughed. "I'm gonna sleep then I'll be here tonight." I placed a hand deliberately on my cock and rubbed it. "If you need anything in the middle of the night... well..." I winked at him.

I knew it would make him angry.

"Come in here in the middle of the night with that thing, and I'll bite it off."

"Ouch," I whispered. "Night, babe. Pleasant dreams."

I knocked on the door. The lock slipped off. "Don't miss me too much."

I closed the door amidst some pretty harsh words.

"Looks like you made an impression," Herman said, locking the door.

Oh, I'd made an impression all right, and as pissed as he was with me, I still felt the heat of his attraction. It sizzled in the air between us, all the anticipated possible things we could do to each other.

I went down to the end of the hallway and crawled into the bed, telling one of the wannabes to wake me at two o'clock.

I dozed a little but didn't sleep well. I was hard as a rock and feeling really horny. I couldn't help but think of Colby all alone in that room down the hallway, and I wondered if I could be seductive enough to get a little forgiveness.

I was out of bed before two, and everyone except the outdoor guards and Chase had gone. When he saw me, he stood. "Okay, cool. I'm outta here. I'll lock up. The guards are out there and will let you know if anyone approaches."

"I'll check on them, then just hang out down here," I said.

"Great." He tossed me a set of keys and walked out.

I walked down the hallway and opened the door at the end. Calvin was fast asleep and snoring on the bed. I locked the door again and travelled down to where Colby was.

When I opened the door, there was a lamp burning on the side table. Colby was sitting up, pillow behind his back. He still had all his clothes on.

"What do you want?" He looked at me.

"You," I said softly.

"If you know what's good for you . . ." he began, but as I came closer, his voice faltered. He looked up at me, and I pulled off my T-shirt. His gaze stayed on my chest. "Don't."

"Don't what?" I asked him. "I won't do anything unless you tell me to."

"Well, you'll stand there a long fuckin' time," he muttered, looking away.

"I don't think so," I replied, unsnapping my jeans and unzipping them.

"What in hell are you doing?" He looked at me again.

"Getting ready for bed. It's two in the morning."

"Well . . . you're . . . not . . ." He stopped because I had pulled my jeans down to my feet. "I need help with my boots."

He looked away again.

I shrugged. "Okay." I toed them off and then stepped out of my jeans. I pushed them away with my foot.

I was in a pair of black briefs, and my cock was already erect. Colby was trying really hard not to notice. He was losing.

I slid my fingers inside the band of my briefs, and Colby's

hand shot out and grabbed mine. "You said you wouldn't."

"Wouldn't what?" I met his gaze.

"Do anything unless I said."

"To you," I corrected. "Didn't say anything about me. If you're not going to touch me, I'll have to do it myself."

"You . . ." He stopped. "It won't change my mind. Do what you want," he shrugged. "And it's risky, isn't it?"

"No." I shook my head. "We're alone, except for the guards outside."

He drew his knees up.

"Got something to hide?"

"No."

"Could be a weapon. I should check."

He looked up at me. "If you touch me, I'll tell Chase."

"He won't believe you." I proceeded to remove the briefs. "Chase has never been inclined to believe anything other than his stereotypes. Unless my voice raises two octaves and my wrists suddenly grow weak, he won't buy that I like cock."

Colby's gaze caressed my erection. I could feel the heat. I could feel his need as urgent as I felt mine. "Don't be cruel," I whispered.

He looked up sharply. "Stroke it."

I took my fully erect cock in my hand, folded my fingers around the shaft, and moved my hand slowly up and down. My breathing got a bit shallow. Just looking at him was enough, even if he was fully dressed.

Colby's tongue wet his lips, and he didn't look away. I saw him press his thighs tighter together. "Move one hand up over your chest."

I did, while I continued to jerk off in front of him. He was killing me. He was killing us both.

"Yeah," he breathed. "Nice. Real nice. Keep caressing your chest like that. It makes your nipples hard and . . .

Goddamnit, you're so . . . ." He grunted and lowered his head.

I stopped touching myself. I reached out and lifted his chin. "Can't you break your fucking rule once?" My finger worked over his lips. I moved up closer to the bed. "Suck it. Take it in your mouth. Make me come. If I can't come inside your ass, then I'll come in your mouth."

I pulled his face closer, and Colby's tongue reached out and licked the head of my cock. I heard that low moan, the one I'd heard before. He was about to drive me out of my mind.

He brought his head back and met my gaze. "Diego," he said softly.

"Say it, say my name and touch me. Touch me," I urged.

His fingertips moved over my shaft. God, it hurt. I was so hard. He lowered his head and licked it, and I grunted. "Stop teasing me and . . . damn it, Colby."

He chuckled softly. "Two can play, right, shit . . ." he breathed, licking the head again. "You are . . . beauty, so male so . . . fucking . . . Damn you, Diego."

That was it. I couldn't take it anymore. I grabbed his shoulders and pressed him down, dragging him to the side of the bed. I opened his mouth and let my cock move into it. He didn't fight me. His hand moved and unzipped his own pants as he took me deeper into his throat. He took out his erection and began to stroke himself.

I watched as he feasted on my cock. My knees were weakening. I cried out as I felt the rush, and he held on, coming at the same time. I stumbled back, away from the bed and Colby doubled up, moaning. His hand still on his cock, he was on his knees, muffling his cries against his sleeve.

My breathing slowed as I paced a little, come running down my thigh. I turned to look at him. I wanted to be inside him so badly. Just the thought of it was making me hard again. But he'd told me no. So it was no.

I watched him as he did up his pants and got off the bed. "I need to wash my hands, sticky," he said.

I reached for my clothes.

He came back out. "You can stay like that if you want. The view is fantastic, much better than the view from this window."

"I'm not here to provide you with a view," I muttered, zipping up my jeans.

"You sound pissed." He sat on the bed.

I reached for my T-shirt.

"I understand," Colby said.

"Do you?" I looked at him. "And just what do you understand?"

"Pretty boys like you are used to getting what they want in bed. When they don't, it hurts their ego."

I stared at him.

"Did I hit a nerve?" His voice sounded so cool all of a sudden. But that's the way he was, hot and cold—most of it an act. But it was getting to me.

"Listen to me," I walked over to the bed. "You don't want to fuck me, fine. Don't. I'm not hurt, my ego is just fine. And I can walk out this door as soon as the babysitting is over and fuck some other guy. And this guy might really appreciate it. I won't have to plead with him to suck my cock. So, you know what? Hang right onto your sacred little oath, and I hope it keeps you warm at night, Colby. As for me, I'm done playing games."

I walked across the floor and reached for the door handle.

"It's a compliment, really," Colby said softly.

I barely heard him. I turned to look at him. "Is that so?"

"Um. Means I could . . ." He stopped. "And that's why," he said under his breath.

I shook my head. "What?"

"If you weren't so dangerous, we could fuck. I'd break the rule if it was just to get off."

I didn't move. "Translate 'dangerous.'"

"I think you know."

I swallowed hard. Yeah, I knew. I forced myself to turn the knob. "You don't have to worry. I'll keep my distance." I opened the door, then paused. "Tell me one thing, did you break the rule with Franklin Kennedy or was he just too dangerous as well?"

I heard him gasp. I walked out and closed the door behind me. I locked it then pressed my forehead against it for a moment. I heard him pacing in there. I was dangerous because he was afraid of caring too much. What in hell did he think he was to me? If someone found us together, it could have gotten me killed.

I was relieved to see Marcel the next morning with donuts and coffee. I grabbed a coffee and told him I was off to get some sleep. I walked over to the office and went inside to see my mom.

"You look like shit," she said.

"Thanks," I told her. "Didn't sleep. I gotta get some. I'm going home to feed the cat."

"Cat?" She scoffed. "You don't have a damn cat. If you did, it would be six feet under by now, poor beast."

I grinned. "Gotta go."

"Scram, kid," she said.

I walked back to where my bike was parked and met Chase.

"Everything good?" he asked.

"Fine. I'm going to sleep. I'll be back."

"Good," he said. He seemed preoccupied. "I'll ah . . . drop by later . . . your place. Got something we need to talk about." He walked away.

I straddled my bike. That was weird. But I forgot about it and chatted with some of the others for a few minutes, aware that Colby was in the window looking down at me.

"We going to keep them locked in those rooms forever?" I asked Nuts, who was still fiddling with his bike.

"Calvin wants to join our club, so we're going to give him a job with the scrap if you don't mind."

I was surprised. "No, it's okay."

"Cledus wants us to take Calvin into the fold. Colby too."

My eyes widened a little. "Cledus?"

"Death Proof is disintegrating, Diego. Cledus is worried about Colby. He wants him to have a family, someone around him like the club, to protect him. He says he's going to talk to Colby and suggest he join the Banni."

"How does Chase feel about all this?"

"Chase owes Cledus a favor, something in the past. He's cool with it."

But I wasn't cool with it, at all. All I needed was Colby in our club with his fucking rules and . . . *Oh damn.*

I glanced up at the window for a second, then away. I put on my helmet and started the engine. I waved to Nuts and drove off.

I had three rooms above a Jazz club on South Boulevard — a bedroom, a small kitchen, and a bathroom. It was all I needed. I was rarely ever there. Chase asked me why I didn't stay at the clubhouse. I couldn't tell him it was because sometimes I wanted a place to fuck. I had a television in my room and a balcony to stand out on when it was suffering hot. It was perfect.

When I got inside the door, I fell face down on my mattress and didn't move for at least ten hours.

Chase woke me up, pounding at my door like a madman. I checked the alarm. It was almost eight o'clock. "Shit." I stumbled out of bed in the dark and went to the door. "Wait a minute." I slid off the lock and saw Chase there.

I left the door open, and he came in, closing it after him. "You were still in bed?"

"Yeah. Don't tell me anything too complicated right now. I'm still asleep."

"You got coffee?"

"No."

"Damn it, Diego. I'll go down and get us some. Take a shower."

He was gone again. I stripped off and took a quick shower. When I came out, dressed in clean jeans, Chase was sitting at the table with coffees. He lit a cigarette. I sat down at the table and grabbed the cup. I took a swig. "What's up?" I looked at him.

"We need to talk about my meeting with the TC."

"I thought you were going to hold church and tell the club before?"

"I was but . . . this concerns you. If you agree, then we'll avoid a lot of shit, and the TC will work out an agreement with us that's fair. I want to bring good news to the table."

"And Spider?"

"He's been given a choice, join us or them."

"So Death Proof is over?"

"Looks like."

"And what does this have to do with me?"

"You met the sergeant at arms for TC, right? And broke his arm?"

I narrowed my eyes. "Yeah. Franklin. Mean fucker. Why?"

"Did you do something else to him, like fuck his ol' lady or something?"

"What?" I laughed. "No."

"He's got a hankering for you, man, and not in a good way."

I couldn't tell Chase, but I knew it had to do with Colby. I'm sure Colby tortured him with his goddamned rule, too, and somehow Franklin knew I'd had Colby. How? Maybe his gaydar was good.

"Diego, he wants to fight you."

"Okay," I shrugged. "Get a hold of three-fingered Fred and we'll set something up."

"No." Chase sighed. "He wants an extreme fight with just the club members present. He's got some strange terms."

"Like?" I lifted an eyebrow.

"Like some heavy punishment for the loser. I'm talking sodomy. Not to the death. He wants you alive. Winner gets to . . . ." He trailed off.

I smiled. "I got the picture."

"Humiliation. I know you can take him, but I don't get why he'd want to do this over a broken arm."

I just shrugged.

"What do you say, man? You can turn it down."

"I like it. Tell him we're on."

"You're my champ," Chase said. He got to his feet and hugged me. "Coming?"

On the street, I said, "Chase, are we really taking Calvin and Colby into the club?"

"They'll start as prospects."

I laughed.

"What?"

"Nothing," I said.

I could just picture Colby being a prospect and obeying orders, especially from me.

"They'll fit in," Chase said. "Let's take the long way. I feel like a ride."

Chase and I rode for a while. It felt good. I felt free. When we drove up to the clubhouse, I sat outside, and that feeling returned. The clubhouse door opened, and some guys walked out. I could have sworn I saw Colby walking around by the bar. I closed my eyes and sighed. More than any extreme fight, it was this that scared me most—Colby joining the Banni.

I got off my bike and called over to Nuts. "Hey," I said, "I swear I saw Colby walking around in there."

"Yeah," Nuts said, popping some cashews in his mouth. "Want a nut?"

I sighed. "No thanks. Looks like I already got one."

CHAPTER SEVEN

Colby

I asked the guys to let me out of the van after fifty or so miles. I begged, actually. Loving the freedom of riding motorbikes as we all did, Dave and Marcel agreed. I think Sue Ellen, who'd been riding the whole way on the back of Nuts' bike might have had some influence, too.

"Don't be any trouble," they said.

"He won't." She winked at Marcel and Dave. "I'll vouch for him."

Truth be told, I kept plotting my escape but was otherwise no trouble, just like I promised.

Then it all changed.

We were at a rest stop three-quarters of the way to Baton Rouge when I received a telephone call from the last person on earth I expected to hear from. Detective Rogan Duchesne, whose name was pronounced the old Southern way, Rouge-an, was on the line. I was still reeling from the last encounter I'd had with Diego. I couldn't believe that comment about Franklin he'd hurled had me. I didn't even know he knew about that.

The call from Duchesne took me out of that for a moment.

"Where you at, Mr. Young?"

"I'm about to get back on the freeway. Almost into Baton Rouge. Where you at?" I couldn't resist throwing the question back at Duchesne.

"I'm at my desk," came back the mild reply. "I'm wondering if you might do me the favor of meeting me for a cup of coffee."

I swallowed the last sip of the disgusting thing that was supposed to pass for coffee I was already drinking. More mud than actual java, it had probably put several hairs on my chest, and I suddenly wondered if Diego liked hairy chests. Then I wondered why I cared. Damn him, he'd pissed me off earlier. I cast a worried glance across the table at my deadpan escorts, Dave and Marcel.

Would they agree to another stop?

Nuts was already preparing to leave with Sue Ellen. She was anxious to reach the city to check on the relocated Jerry.

"When?" I asked into the phone, giving her and Nuts a wave as they took off.

Damn it. The truth was Duchesne only ever contacted me when he had an update on Garnet Beauty. She was the only thing in the world that mattered at this moment in time. Emotion pricked at the back of my eyes.

"Do you have news?" I asked, aware of Marcel's glance on my face.

"We haven't found her if that's what you're asking, but I do need your permission on something, since you're the self-appointed family spokesman. I woulda called June Gold, but she about falls apart as soon as she hears my voice."

"I'll be there." That was so typical of June. She couldn't handle the past, and I'd always suspected there were things that went on that she hadn't told me. I contemplated stealing one of the many motorbikes outside the Kream Kaffé, one of the ubiquitous rest stops along the 10 freeway. The long stretch between Texas and Louisiana had been nothing but roadkill. Everything from farm animals to kittens lay dead along the shoulder. A macabre welcome back to the land of my home.

We'd ridden almost seven hours, and every bone in my

body ached. "Just say when and where."

"Rumor has it you're joining the Banni."

I couldn't believe my ears. "How do you know that?"

"I'm a detective, Mr. Young. Rumor also has it you're under protection of the Banni. And ah, I suppose you know there's a quarter of a million-dollar bounty on you?"

I'm worth that much to . . . anybody? "You lookin' to collect a quick payday?" I couldn't resist asking. I have no idea why I needle this guy so much. Garnet's disappearance had bothered him as much as it did me all these years. He was in his late thirties, ten years older than me. We'd been in touch since he caught Garnet's case a month after Cledus first reported her missing. With the passage of time, between her disappearance and Cledus alerting the authorities, she wound up in the homicide division's clutches.

Duchesne had been a fresh cop, twenty-two to my twelve. Now that I thought about it, I was damned lucky he was a detective who cared.

He'd seen too much violent crime, yet he was a man who still had a heart. When a little kid in the Florida parish got killed in a hit and run a couple of years ago, it was Duchesne and his team who coughed up the dough for his funeral and a decent headstone. I don't even have a grave for my sister. Her vanishing is a hole in my life. A hole that keeps getting dug at, but there are no human remains.

"I would prefer to see you alive rather than dead, believe it or not, even though you're such an asshole," Duchesne said.

I laughed because it was true. I was often rude to him because I feared bad news. I feared the worst each time I heard his goddamned voice. I should have been kinder to him because he was the only person alive who knew and understood, my anguish over Garnet. Not even June was as obsessed as I.

111

Duchesne was always sympathetic, and even though he had a huge roster of homicides to work on, I knew I could walk into his office, and Garnet Beauty's photo would be on his wall, right where he could see her every single day.

Although it was kinda fun bantering, I worried about my cell phone battery petering out. It had one bar of juice left. I was surprised it still worked, actually.

"Where do you want to meet, Detective?"

"Magpie Café," he said. "Best you keep headin' to Baton Rouge. Skip New Orleans for now, though I bet you're tempted to check on your sister's kids.

"It's on the Perkins Road overpass. Your companions will know it. They won't like cutting you loose, so bring 'em with. I'll be there in half an hour."

He ended the call, and I glanced up at Marcel, whose stone-faced gaze remained on my face.

"Did I just hear you say detective?"

I winced, putting the cell phone back into my pocket and slinging my messenger bag back around my body. It had begun to get heavy over the long ride. "Yeah."

"You're friendly with the police?"

"Naw. It's . . . oh, shit. It's family business."

"Family business?" Marcel looked like a biker through-and-through. He even had Banni insignia on his tattooed hands. Would he understand?

I held his gaze. "My sister disappeared a long time ago. He's helping me look for her. He needs me to sign some papers."

"That's a likely story." Dave dropped his empty cup into the saucer. I noticed the waitress cutting a glance at our table. "You some kind of informant?"

"What the fuck?" I stared at him. "No. I'm no informant. And now I need a ride to the Magpie Café. He's meeting me there in half an hour."

The two men looked at each other. "No funny business," Marcel said, surprising me by grabbing me by the throat. I hadn't seen him produce the knife now in his free hand. He flicked me with it, for no other reason than to prove his intentions. I badly wanted to beat the shit out of him. I grabbed a couple of paper napkins and pressed them to my throat. The bastard. I was bleeding all over the place. I couldn't believe the pain a small nick could cause.

That was when I made out the writing on the backs of all his fingers.

DEATH HURTS.

Okey dokey then.

Outside, a sudden, chill wind whipped at me. The blood on my throat wouldn't stop running, and it pissed me off that Marcel was so pleased to have cut me. I asked to ride behind Dave.

"Why?" Marcel asked.

"Because I'm in danger of pushing you off the damned bike. I don't care if I kill us both."

He looked surprised. Asshole.

We rode into East Baton Rouge, arriving a few minutes late for my appointment with Duchesne. As we roared along Perkins Road, I noticed the sign for Parrain's Seafood Restaurant to my right. Its daily special had been stenciled onto a huge billboard out front. Catfish Chenier. My stomach rumbled at the thought of the rich, creamy, Creole shrimp sauce.

Come to think of it, I remembered the sign and the daily special. Last time I'd passed by here, the same special was being advertised. As we stopped the bikes next door and I got off Dave's ride, I was pleased to see when I took the napkin away from my throat from under the helmet strap, that the small knife wound had stopped bleeding.

I looked around. Zippy's burrito bar stood on the other

side of the brown, weathered wooden house that was the Magpie Café. That was the only thing out of place. The building seemed familiar to me, but not the name. Wait. I remembered it now. It had been a weird and unsuccessful merger of a tattoo parlor and hair salon last time I'd come here.

Fuck.

How could I have forgotten?

I mentally shook my head. I'd visited Franklin Kennedy here once when he was helping out his brother's failing business. He'd started working as a tattoo artist working at the Perkins Road Parlor. Business had been damned slow, and Franklin and his brother's partners had been freaking. I'd been nervous it might have been a bad idea to visit him when he'd asked me to come by, but I'd kinda liked the guy. I'd even brought Sue Ellen, Jerry's mom, and treated her to a new hairdo while I chatted with Franklin.

For me, any man who tried to help his family—as I did my own sister in her business—deserved some support. Jerry had flipped out because he thought we were patronizing the enemy.

And now that enemy wanted me dead, and I was a damned hostage of the Banni!

I stared at the sign, recalling the simple red one that had previously adorned the shingles. Salon, it had read. Clearly, it had gone belly-up. What had happened to the motley crew Franklin had been working with? And if the business had gone bust, where the hell had he found a quarter of a million bucks to place a bounty on me?

Franklin. Ugh. This had to be some sort of retaliation. The guy was some kind of stalker. And that was another story . . .

The Magpie looked busy. Happy sounds of chattering could be heard from where we stood. "You comin' in?" I asked Dave and Marcel.

"No, thanks." Marcel spat at the ground. "I'm allergic to cops."

"Suit yourself."

I strolled inside, adjusting my messenger bag on my shoulder. I loved the smell of jambalaya I got as soon as I walked through the door. I could hardly keep the saliva in my mouth. Drool just wanted to pour out of it. I saw Duchesne lift a hand in greeting from a corner table and I made my way over to him. He had a big cappuccino in front of him. Ah. Decent coffee had finally reached Baton Rouge.

He stood, and we shook hands, his gaze on my throat. "Who cut you?" His expression turned pained.

"No biggie." I took a seat opposite him at the table for four. Two extra seats by the window. He'd planned for my escorts to be here.

"The jambalaya here is excellent," he said. "You look like you could use a feed."

He wasn't kidding. Apart from the mud I'd drunk on the road, I couldn't remember the last time I'd actually eaten any food.

The waitress took our orders. I asked for a cappuccino.

"You'll love it," she assured me.

I didn't need her to tell me that, but I appreciated her confidence, especially since I noticed her stepping behind the counter to make it herself. I wondered if the Banni would appreciate my lunch break.

"You okay?" Duchesne asked me. He looked the same as ever—good-looking in a straight kinda way—dark hair, solid build, warm brown eyes that always made me think of milk-chocolate chips.

"I'm fine." I added, "Thanks for asking."

"I heard what happened to Jerry McGraw. I heard the Banni moved him out of the hospital. I hope he's gonna be okay, Colby. I know he's like a brother to you."

He made me squirm in my seat. I guess me and Jerry are like brothers. More like kissing cousins—or formerly screwing cousins. As soon as our meeting was over, I'd check up on him. *Damn it.* I'd have to call my father, too.

"I have some news." Duchesne adopted his I-mean-business look.

"You said you haven't found Garnet Beauty." Sometimes just saying her name relieved all kinds of pressure for me. She was the weight in my heart and my soul.

"No, but recently my department got some extra funds to work on some cold cases. I've been in touch with a few . . . well, several law enforcement agencies all here in the South. Far too many Jane Does have been buried over the years. Far too many families left hangin' in the wind." He looked up suddenly. "Hello." I glanced up, not too surprised to see Dave and Marcel hovering over me.

"We gotta get movin'." Dave stared daggers at me. He looked stunned when my food arrived. He envied my coffee; I could tell.

"Sit down," Duchesne said. "He ain't goin' nowhere yet."

Something in his tone seemed to make those boys' knees buckle, and they moved beside us. Marcel took the seat next to mine, which dimmed my pleasure in the delicious-looking bowl of food that awaited me.

"Is that jambalaya?" Marcel asked

"Is that a cappuccino?" Dave asked.

Soon, they'd each ordered both. They looked around the café, and Duchesne resumed his speech.

"There are a few buried Jane Does and three remains left in cold storage that could be your sister." Duchesne shuffled a few papers around. I became aware of Dave and Marcel's gazes on my face.

"I thought your sister owned a bakery in N'Orleans,"

Marcel said.

"Different sister." I hated this weirdo knowing my business.

Duchesne acted as though the intrusion hadn't occurred. "There are two burials that could be Garnet Beauty." He opened up a folded piece of paper.

"This little girl was so badly decomposed when the authorities discovered her in Alabama that they couldn't really take photos of her to distribute to the public. They hired a sketch artist to do a drawing of what they think she looked like." He pushed the paper toward me.

Hope skipped in my heart until I saw the picture. Nothing like her.

"Alabama?" I asked.

"It's only a six-and-a-half hour drive. Whoever did this could have driven the body there."

"When was this?" It was hard to eat when we were discussing my Garnet.

"This little girl was only discovered five years ago, but she was found in a water cooler tossed into some woods. She'd been there a long time. Time frame could fit. Reason I wanted to see you is that there are two bodies, two graves that could also fit. The other one's in Georgia. Both states are willing to dig up their Jane Does so that we can run DNA tests. To do that, both are requesting a signature from family members for permission."

I dropped the spoon I'd just picked up and signed his multiple forms.

"Anything," I said. "Anything you need." I looked him in the eye. "Thank you." I was in danger of bawling. Had someone really stuffed a little girl into a cooler and thrown her away like trash?

Had this person done it to my Garnet?

"She means a lot to me, too," Duchesne said. I already

knew part of his quest for truth and justice was that his own sister had disappeared several years ago. She had been a model student until she'd discovered LSD and apparently took time off to hitchhike with a friend out to California. The two women argued in Nevada and Duchesne's sister, Lark, called her family from the town of Wells, saying she was coming home. She said she had a ride and expected to be back the following day.

Nobody has ever heard from her again. Rogan went nuts out in the desert, trying to find her. He fell apart badly. I remember the first time I saw him when he came back after a fruitless month hunting for her.

"I'm just never going to be happy again," he told me. "This will haunt me for the rest of my life."

We are in so many ways, kindred spirits. I understand him exactly. It's how I feel about my sister. He has had it rough, too. A serial killer admitted to taking LSD with her and then killing her after a bad trip. He's spent years in prison admitting all kinds of murders but keeps playing with authorities. Duchesne was permitted to interview him, although he is not allowed to actually work the case.

One little detail has him convinced Johnny Masters knew Lark.

She had a distinctive orange sleeping bag, and Lark said he tossed it—and the dead girl—into a ravine out in an old mine off the 80 freeway in Elko County.

So far, the police can officially tie him to one homicide, so at least he's off the streets. He claims not to remember which mine he dumped Lark's body in—or any of the other women he's admitted to killing—but is quick to claim responsibility for dozens of homicides.

Some cops believe the guy is a liar. Duchesne, however, firmly believes Johnny Masters is the man who murdered his sister.

The serial killer is still in the joint and occasionally taunts authorities with clues that go nowhere. Each new outreach just reopens the Duchesne's family's tormented doubts about Lark's vanishing.

As soon as I finished signing the forms, the detective smiled, stuffing them into a fan-folder. When the check came, he grabbed it, which surprised me.

"Your sister sends me cakes every month. I owe you guys."

That was a surprise. June wouldn't talk to him, but sent him cakes? He rose from the table. "I'll be in touch, Colby."

As he moved away from us, he whipped around, snapping his fingers. "Oh, one more thing." His eyes turned dark as he glanced from Marcel to Dave.

"You take care of this man. If anything happens to him, I'll hold you accountable. And if I see any more cuts on him, I'll haul you into the can so fast, your heads'll spin."

And with that, he slapped some money on the counter with the check and split.

Neither of the Banni said anything for a moment.

"When did your sister disappear?" Marcel finally asked.

"A long time ago, when I was about nine. I didn't find out until I was twelve. That was fifteen years ago." I didn't tell them they'd lived right here in East Baton Rouge, in the Florida parish. Coming here wasn't exactly fun for me.

My cell phone rang again. I checked the readout, surprised to see it was Duchesne.

I took the call. "Yes, Detective?"

"I didn't want to say anything to you in front of your goons, but I want you to put a little pressure on your sister when you can. I'm convinced she knows more than she's ever let on. Now is the time. Anything she can tell us . . ." His voice drifted away. "She'll only tell you. I'm sure of it."

I was convinced of both things, too. I hadn't put pressure

on my sister because the subject of Garnet hurt us both so much. I stared at Marcel's hands. I think in that moment, I knew. I was finally certain. Our baby was dead.

And fuck. He was right.

Death hurts.

Marcel and Dave took me to some kind of Banni crash pad behind what turned out to be Diego's custom bike-building business. The crash pad was a two-story house that wasn't bad, but it wasn't the Hilton Hotel, either. The place looked pretty clean as Marcel, Dave, and I walked inside. I noticed the husks of some kind of nuts all over the floor.

Marcel shook his head. "Aw, Nuts."

"You rang?" Nuts came out of nowhere, clutching a huge bag of sunflower seeds. He kept up a constant pattern of pouring the seeds into his hand, tossing back his head and throwing them into his mouth. One by one, the husks emerged as he spat them into his fist, then dropped them to the floor.

Lovely.

"Keep an eye on him." Marcel gestured to me. And with that, he and Dave walked out the door again.

Nuts looked about as thrilled with his new assignment as I felt. I wondered how long it would take before I could shake him loose. Time was a-wasting. I wanted to visit my sister and put a little heat under her ass, and then I wanted to talk to my father and Calvin. Well, maybe not in that order.

Calvin. Where the hell was he? Where was Jerry?

"I need to make some calls," I told Nuts. "My cell phone's about of juice. Is there a phone I can use?"

Nuts spat some husks from his fist to the floor, one eye on a giant plasma TV mounted to the wall above a sectional so-fa, the other swiveling to the living room where I noticed a laptop propped on a huge dining table.

"There's a landline there. Who you callin'?"

"My dad. I haven't spoken to him. Any idea where Calvin is?"

"Yeah. Upstairs sleeping."

I'll bet. "When did you last check in on him?"

"What?" He projected a handful of seed husks to the floor and shook some more seeds into his mouth. "You don't trust me?"

"I trust you." It's Calvin I don't trust. "What about Jerry?"

Nuts pulled a face, chomped around his mouthful some, then spat out a few husks. It was gross to watch this stuff.

"He's in a convalescent hospital. My aunt is a nurse there, and they don't ask too many questions."

"That was nice of you to organize that," I said, starting to revise my opinion of Nuts.

Ptht, ptht. Husks dropped to the floor. "Wasn't me. Diego organized it. I hate the bitch." He turned away from me and switched on the TV. I watched for a moment. It was an episode of Paranormal Witness in which an Italian priest tried to drive demons from a young woman's body.

It freaked me out. I actually got scared watching that shit. I turned to walk up the stairs, and Nuts suddenly asked, "You know the expression 'everybody has their demons'?"

"Yeah." I turned back to him. "I do."

"Well, I finally understand it. Everybody does. Some people have anger. That's the name of an actual demon, you know."

I didn't want to have this discussion. I'd read somewhere once that demons actually attacked people who researched them. A demon called Anger? No way would I look that up anywhere online.

"We all got our demons." Ptht, ptht. "What's yours?" He seemed curious.

"I don't know. What about you?"

"Numerous ones." Ptht, ptht. He turned back to the TV again. *Holy crap.* I had to get outta this house. I climbed the stairs and found Calvin lying on a bed in the second room I checked.

Stretched out, hands under his head, he looked like he didn't have a care in the world, but I knew better.

"What the fuck?" He sat up, swinging his legs down to the floor. "I've been waitin' here forever, and you stop to have lunch with that cock tease, Duchesne?"

Calvin was convinced Duchesne was gay and that he sniffed around the Young men, his Young man in particular, using his dormant investigation as a ruse. If Rogan Duchesne was gay, he'd never let on to me. We never talked about our personal lives. I thought about the papers I'd signed. I didn't want to get into that with Calvin. His animosity toward the detective was another reason Duchesne tended to reach out to me these days instead of my father.

"Where's Cledus at?" he asked.

"No idea. Don't you know?"

He frowned at me. "I bet he's visitin' that idiot friend of yours."

"Jerry?"

"You know any other idiots?"

From downstairs, I could hear the faint sound of demonic voices from the TV and the awful ptht, ptht. Yeah. I know a few idiots.

"I should go check on him." I eyed Calvin's cell phone charging on the bedside table.

"Can I use your phone? I need to charge mine."

"Not to call your cheatin' ass friend, you can't."

Okey dokey then. Geez. This plan of protection with the Banni was turning out to be all kinds of fun . . .

"I could turn your ass over to the TCs. Run off with all the money," he said.

Sure. He said it as a joke, but it wasn't too damned funny. And I always think behind every barbed joke is a savage truth. I was on Calvin's shit list. I turned and walked out of there. I'd had enough of his bullshit.

Downstairs in the living room, the Italian priest was in his cellar throwing Holy water on an old lady who sat in a chair, shrieking. When she flew to the ceiling, and the chair started ricocheting around the room, I averted my gaze.

"Where's Diego?" I asked.

Ptht, ptht. "In the chop shop. Not sure you're s'pose to be runnin' around out there, though."

"I'll go right inside." Did he think he'd been assigned to supervise me to the extent he'd be watching every move I made? Would this job involve him wiping my ass?

"I'm watchin' you." Ptht, ptht.

"Perfect." I picked up my messenger bag, dropping some of my stuffed clothes onto a chair to lighten my load. He watched me the whole time. I walked over to the back door. "Thanks." Ptht, ptht. I mimicked spitting into my hand. He actually grinned.

Outside, I inhaled a hunk of warm air. The house had smelled stale. I would go bonkers spending too much time in there. I hustled over to the bike shop where the sounds of laughter and mechanical activity gave me hope that I wouldn't go out of my mind . . . yet.

I turned as I walked through the back screen door of the bike shop. Nuts hadn't been lying. He was watching me. I didn't know whether to feel reassured or really worried.

And then I saw Diego in overalls, kneeling beside a bike, working on finishing its paint job. He had an artist's hand, that's for sure. He'd painted on flames along the rim, the graphics airbrushed to give the finished product a 3D effect. It was amazing.

He stood, turned and looked at me, lifting his goggles to his head.

"You doin' okay?"

"What do you care?" I asked, but I was struck by the amazing work going on around me. I cleared my throat. Maybe I should try to be on the good side of him. Catch more flies with honey. "This is some setup you got here."

"Thanks." He gave me a crooked, half-smile, and damn him, it went straight to my cock. Hard to tear my gaze away from his gorgeous face even if he did piss me off, but I had to. He picked up his coffee cup, taking a swig. I thought about the places on my body that his tongue had been. That was my problem. I wanted it right back there again.

I took a step back and bumped into someone.

"Sorry," I said until I realized it was a bike frame.

"Only you would apologize to an inanimate object." Diego's tone was teasing, but tender. "Do you want me to show you around?"

It surprised me that he was being so nice, but as we went from one room to the next, his very professional operation impressed me. Finally alone, he stole the moment to say, "You never told me about your sister."

I shrugged. Damn. That was the shoulder injury. She was my burden. My handicap. Whenever Duchesne called me, the pain flared again. I'd gotten drunk with a couple of the Australian bikers last year, and one of them talked about his own burden. He was part Aborigine, and he told me his people had a special word for the burden of a child.

Shiralee.

And now those mo-fos were trying to kill me.

"They're digging her up?" he asked, his concern appearing real.

"We've never found her, and Detective Duchesne wants permission to dig up the graves of a couple of Jane Does. I

124

gave it to him."

Diego studied me intently. "Marcel said you had to sign papers. Is he making your family responsible for paying for this?"

Man, that had never occurred to me. I blinked in concentration, then shook my head. "He never mentioned it. I think he would have. Even if I had to give him my last dime, Garnet Beauty is worth it."

"Garnet Beauty. Is that her name?"

Shit. I just nodded.

"If there is a cost involved, the Banni will help." He squeezed my shoulder. The bad one. I almost screamed out in agony. "We may be all kinds of assholes around here, but we're partial to families. Especially children."

He released me, and the pain in my shoulder washed down my back. It was as though he'd lit a match to my flesh.

Would she ever stop hurting me?

"I'm sorry about your sister," he said, his tone soft. "You wanna see some cool bikes? Then I'll take you to see Jerry. Your dad's with him. He doesn't trust any of us to watch over him."

God. No wonder Calvin was so pissed.

It took everything in me not to say, "No, I'd rather roll around naked in bed with you."

Instead, I gave him a smile. "Show me everything."

CHAPTER EIGHT

In spite of the fact that I wasn't happy about being a virtual prisoner of the Banni, I was seriously impressed by the array of bikes on display and was surprised to see some bikes I'd coveted at motorbike shows in glass cases in strategic places around the shop floor. The space was deceptively huge and a loving homage to the world I adored. I stopped dead in front of a motorbike I'd coveted for years.

"My God," I said, touching the glass house around it. "Is that a Britten V-one thousand?"

"It is." He grinned, folding his arms in front of his chest. "You know your bikes."

I shook my head. "This is a thing of sheer genius—and beauty. How'd you get it?"

"He gave it to me." His voice turned quiet, and I could barely hear him above the noises in the shop.

I almost fell on the floor. "John Britten gave you this bike? But he's been dead . . . what, seventeen years?"

He nodded. "Worst day of my life. The most passionate, innovative motorbike builder in the world, dead at forty-five."

"He was a New Zealander. How did you meet him?"

"In Daytona. I was a kid. Nineteen ninety-five. And I—"

"Holy shit. You went to that race!"

"I did. I hitchhiked. He made history that year at the Daytona Twins, taking first and second place. He broke records."

That made me smile. "Yeah. And he shocked everybody

finishing forty-three seconds ahead of the two Harley super-bikes and the latest model Bimota and Ducati V-twins." He was rocking on his feet now. The joy of talking to a kindred spirit ignited his own passion, I could tell.

"What was he like?" I couldn't believe Diego had met my hero.

"He was the most humble man I've ever met. I wormed my way into his crew's pit. For three days I learned everything I could from him. He was a kind man—and a fucking—absolutely fucking genius. He freaked out everybody by designing a bike that beat a Harley!"

Diego pointed to the bike's seat. "He developed the innovative use of carbon fiber, a fabric which—up until he came along—was more commonly used in the construction of yachts and ski-boots. It gave the bike extra speed on the racetrack, due to its lightness and strength.

"See here? A beam is bolted to the top of the cylinders and stretched out to hold the saddle. Attached to the front of the engine is a modernized version of girder forks, which sit upright, attached to a swinging arm by a long connecting rod, giving the bike an almost intuitive sense of the road. Nothing in the world like it."

He seemed in a trance now.

"And he gave you this bike?" I couldn't get past this fact. What I was looking at was a museum piece. In fact, there is a Britten bike on display in a museum somewhere, but there's always been controversy about whether it was a real racing bike or a 'shadow bike' created from factory parts.

"When I met him, it was February. He had an intensity to him I've never encountered before. He wouldn't sleep. His enthusiasm was contagious. He'd studied birds, you know. He was quite the expert. He wanted to create faster, even more beautiful, bikes. He was so keen to share his knowledge. He taught me something I hold valuable to this day. He taught me that one man, with a dream, and the right team, can build his own bikes."

He swept his hand around the shop. "He called himself a backyard builder, and I'm proud to carry on that tradition." He looked emotional for a moment. "He encouraged me. We talked on the phone after he went back home. He sent me letters with ideas. Suggestions." He closed his eyes. "I wanted to go apprentice for him. I had no idea he was dying. I guess he saw me as his last-ditch effort to make a step into the international marketplace. I will never, ever understand why God chose to give that man aggressive melanoma and take him from this life. I often wonder what he could have made, given more time."

His face took a mystical expression. "I bet he could have made a machine that could fly."

I let him settle with that thought for a moment. "Have you taken her for a ride?"

He laughed. "Once. If you know about this bike, you know the sound is deafening."

"I read somewhere that somebody described it as 'apocalyptic.'"

He laughed, too. "It's true. It's not a street bike. But one day, we'll take her out." He gazed at the bike. "He left it to me in his will. It was never in a race. It's a shadow bike. But he built it himself. He wanted me to remember that men must be allowed to feel they can fly."

I thought about the flames I'd seen on some of his bikes. His own version of flight, I supposed. Wheels of flame.

"Why are you smiling?" he asked.

"I just remembered reading that someone said that you could always smell burning rubber with a Britten."

He gave me an appreciative look. "It's true."

"So the flames you put on your bikes are an homage to him."

"Very good." He gave me a small clap. "I can see you, and I are going to get along very well." He looked up at a wall clock. "You want to go check on Jerry?"

"I'd like that very much," I said, wondering if he'd let me go visit my sister at some point. Maybe I could talk him into taking me there. It would be just over an hour's ride . . .

Diego drove me to the hospital on one of his custom-made bikes. It hugged the road like a dream, and I hugged his ass and hips like he was the last man on earth. With the wind whipping my face, I kept chiding myself.

Don't fall in love. Don't fall in love. Don't fall in love.

The ride was all too short, which was probably a good thing. I was worried about getting a hard-on as I watched him get off that bike and strut toward the entrance of the Corden Rehabilitation Center.

"I should tell you that Jerry's not even registered here," Diego said, over his shoulder. I was sure he could tell I was checking out his ass. I reluctantly let my gaze travel upward. "We've sneaked him into a room. I got Nuts to call in a favor."

"One that I will have to repay, no doubt."

"For sure."

We exchanged smiles as I caught up with him. I could smell the unpleasant combination of illness and antiseptic floor wash that I always associated with hospitals. We walked right past the nurses' station, made a left, and strode past several rooms, where I couldn't resist peeking into open doors, checking out the sick people.

We came to a room near the end. The door was closed. Diego gave a series of short raps, and a hairy-face looked out of a small glass window in the door. The man let us in. I recognized him as a Banni but couldn't recall his name. I spied Jerry lying in bed, half-reclining, with pillows propped under his head and shoulders.

"So, you finally came to see me." His tone was unfriendly, and I caught the apologetic glance from his mother. She stood near the window, my father beside her. He looked a little unkempt, which surprised me. His hair, normally slicked back to disguise the bald patch right on the top of his head, was all flyaway. He wore grimy looking jeans, work boots, and a red-checked shirt he must have bought from the reject bin at Goodwill.

Cledus's hair had turned gray when he was thirty. He'd left it that way. He thought it gave him a Sam Elliott look. I thought it gave him a stupid asshole look.

"Took your sweet time," he said.

I didn't respond. I felt bad I hadn't brought Jerry any flowers or snacks, but he seemed to have plenty of both. And he had enough sympathy for himself to do all of us standing in that room proud.

Jerry stared at my empty hands. "What, you didn't bring me anything?"

I fixed him with my best warning look as he munched from a box of Aunt Sally's Creole Pecan Pralines.

"There's a bounty on my head. I'm not exactly hittin' the hot spots around here, Jerry."

That seemed to piss him off even more. He never could take an injury of any sort. I remember seeing him wail like a little girl one time he got a splinter in his right index finger. I had to sit on him while Sue Ellen extracted the thing with her best tweezers.

I would have let him whine a little, but his fury was apparently mounting.

"So you're the reason I got stabbed," he said.

"No, Jerry. I'm not the asshole who was two-timing your girlfriend." I let my gaze swivel toward my father. "Didn't you think she was gonna go berserk when she found out you're a switch hitter?"

His eyes looked like they were about to pop out of his head. "I'm not a switch hitter!"

"Oh. What do you call it then? Confused?"

He huffed and puffed, trying to sit up straight in the bed. "I never fucked her."

"Come on, Jer. You expect me to believe that?"

He flushed an unflattering shade of crimson. "I told her I was waiting until we got married."

Everyone in the room stared at him.

"No wonder she's pissed," Sue Ellen muttered.

"Well, I was waiting," Jerry said, shooting a nervous glance at my dad. "You couldn't get me drunk enough to bang her. I figured after we were married, I could divorce her and get me some of her moolah."

I stared at him.

"How'd you figure that?" Diego sounded incredulous.

Jerry shrugged. "She's rich! She's loaded. She's got all these secret grows stashed all over the state."

He saw our shocked expressions. "How was I to know she was in thick with the TCs? I'm beginning to think she wants me outta the way because I found some of those properties. I paid for four of the raw lots we use for the grows." He seemed agitated now. "I was the one that hired the trucks with the special soil. I was the one that found the illegal immigrants willing to work night and day, protecting the crops."

Oh, God. My stupid, dumbass friend had gotten himself involved with something way out of his league. He was out of his depth with no clue, no paddle. No fucking brains.

"These properties are in your name?" I asked.

"Both our names." He had the grace to look sheepish. "She wants them all to herself." Jerry looked indignant. "I don't think that's fair, trying to bump me off when I'm the one that's taken responsibility for everything. I'm the one that got rid of the two DEA agents that started sniffing around the property near her house."

"You did . . . what?" I couldn't believe what I was hearing.

"Sure. I had to. Two of my guards at the grow shot 'em, and I burned up their bodies—"

"Stop. I don't want to hear any more. You've become somebody I don't know anymore. You never told me any of this!" I hated bringing up all of this in front of the others, but he was pissing me off. Each new thing he told me was increasingly bad. Boy, how dumb could he be? What the hell made him get involved in all this shit in the first place?

Before I could ask, he said, "She told me she'd make me a rich man. She said within a year I'd never have to work again."

"Being dead, of course, you wouldn't." I became aware of an odd sound and turned to the wall facing Jerry's bed. I was surprised to see a man lying on another hospital bed. His eyes were open, his expression vacant.

"That's Kevin," Jerry said, his voice turning soft. "He's in a coma."

I watched Kevin, wondering what he was doing. I'd never seen a coma patient moving around before. Never seen one with his eyes open like this. His arms were moving in a strange crawl pattern, a strangled cry escaping his throat.

"They do cross-patterning exercises on him twice a day," Sue Ellen said. "They teach him to crawl. Four people come in here and make his arms and legs crawl. Just like a baby. Except it's not working."

"How long has he been here?" It was disturbing, watching and listening to poor Kevin. He was good-looking, with dark hair and huge green eyes, but very thin and pale.

"Eight months. He was in a car accident—head-on collision, hit by a drunk driver. Hit and run, actually." Sue Ellen was stroking Jerry's hair from his eyes when I turned back to look at her.

I glanced at Diego. "Is Kevin a Banni member?"

He shook his head. "Nope. No gang affiliations at all. We've been lucky that Kevin here has no family that's local. He's got a brother in Kentucky, but he stopped visiting months ago. According to Nuts' aunt, who helped us bring Jerry here, the brother is back home working with a lawyer to sue the city of Baton Rouge and its police force for a lot of money. Millions. You can bet, come trial time, he'll be here boo-hooin' like a motherfucker, raking up sympathy from the potential jury pool. By then, Jerry won't be in here anymore."

I turned back to look at Kevin. "Is his life worth millions?"

"Kevin's apparently a famous opera singer," Sue Ellen interjected. "He and his company were on tour here. They all took off for Europe, and his brother just sees a way to make a big hunka cash."

"At least you have visitors—people who care," my father told Jerry.

Jerry wore an expression that said, I'd rather have cash.

To me, Cledus said, "Can we have a word? Privately?"

I glanced at Diego, who seemed to be in some silent battle with my father.

"Don't go far," he said to me.

Cledus and I walked out into the corridor, closing the door behind us.

"So. There's a bounty out on you, and it may or may not have something to do with the fact that Teresa feels her honor has been betrayed. What have they got against you?" my father asked.

"I don't know. I gotta be honest. It may be the TC guy I fooled around with some, a year or so back."

My father stared at me, his eyes narrowed. "That's the rumor. Franklin Kennedy's tellin' everyone you hit on him."

I snorted. "Yeah, right."

"He says he wants your punk ass taken out. You know how they feel about gays in the gangs, Colby. What the fuck were you thinking?"

I held my temper and counted several beats. "I don't know, Pa. What were you thinking when you started banging Jerry?"

"He makes me feel young. Calvin and I fight all the time. He doesn't turn me on anymore."

"Christ. Too much information." I waved off the rest of his words.

He shrugged. "You asked."

"What are you gonna do about your prostate cancer?"

He rolled his eyes. "Told you about that, did he?"

"Calvin loves you. He wants you to be okay."

"I'm fightin' it." He pointed to his forehead. "With this."

Oh, brother.

"Nobody's more strong-minded than me, son."

That was true. Before I could come up with a stinging response, he said, "I know you, and I have had our differences, but I do love you. I don't want anything to happen to you."

I couldn't say the same thing back to him. I didn't want to lie. I wanted to hate him.

"Look, there's things you need to know."

I stared at him. "Like what?"

He looked rattled when he said, "Our club's for shit. It won't be safe for you to go back to your pool hall or your apartment for a long time." He hesitated.

"Go on."

"Bones and Mega have pledged allegiance to the TCs."

That surprised me. They'd been strong Death Proof members for a long time.

"What about the prospects?"

"I don't trust any of 'em. For now, there are five of us core members over here with the Banni. Don't go anywhere alone. Kennedy wants you bad—dead or alive. If they take you alive, you know they'll torture you for days." His expression turned agonized. "There's something I shoulda told you a long time ago."

What now?

"I always had a hunch that Garnet Beauty was abducted by a rival gang for something I did. I wasn't always a good guy. I ran a fearsome gang before you and Jerry turned all gooey and soft on me."

"Is that how you see us?" I shook my head.

"No. I don't. Others do. I'm gonna get Jerry away from here soon as I can. His bitch girlfriend wants him dead. I want him alive. Maybe I can talk Calvin into getting outta here with us."

"Which leaves me alone." Again, naturally.

"You're a survivor," he said.

"Fuck you, Cledus."

"Love you, too, son." He turned on his heel and almost collided with Diego, who was leaning against the wall. I had no idea how long he'd been there, but he looked at my father with an expression of total disgust.

"Let's ride," Diego said to me. I heard my father go back into the room. I heard laughter, but all I could think of was the comatose man in the other bed, swimming to nowhere with his agitated crawl pattern. How much of Jerry's conversation did he understand? How much would he remember?

We rode along the streets. It was starting to get dark. We'd missed some rain, and the asphalt was wet and slippery.

"Where to?" I asked.

"Gotta stop at a club," he shouted over his shoulder.

Fair enough. Maybe I could talk him into going to New Orleans under cover of night. I was worried about my sister. I didn't know why, but I suspected it was my father's comment about Garnet. I didn't believe her disappearance had anything to do with his gang affiliation, but what did I know?

It worried me that I couldn't even call June Gold once we stopped because my cell phone was back at the Banni house charging. I'd ask Diego to lend me his.

We stopped in an industrial section of town, where the only thing open appeared to be a burger stand on the corner. A flat, brown warehouse-type building had a motorbike parked out front. We pulled beside it, and Diego stopped the engine.

I was beginning to hate all the moments I had to take my hands off him.

We walked to the building. He jangled his keys in his hand and unlocked the door. I heard the powerful beat of music, surprise rendering me speechless as we walked inside.

A huge, dark ceiling looking like a moonlit sky with clouds and tiny stars dominated the space.

I could see some guys in there, some dancing, other standing by the bar drinking.

"What is this?" I asked, staring up at the sky, so real-looking it took me a minute to decide it wasn't.

"My new club. Guess what it's going to be called?"

I shook my head. I wanted to be naked with him under that moon—naked, sweaty, and drinking.

"Artificial Moonlight."

I tore my gaze away from the roof. "I like it. You've found a new purpose for that expression."

"Thanks to you."

Our gazes locked.

"The ceiling is amazing," I said.

"Cost me a fortune. Looks real, doesn't it?"

"Very real."

"It's in the bathroom, too."

I swallowed hard, said nothing, but I could feel the sexual heat flaring between us. I could also sense his hesitation. I know I'd put up a front before, refusing him, so I understood his demeanor.

I followed him to the can, surprised to see a motorbike on the middle of the dance floor.

I laughed when I realized it was a Jesse James.

"She's called Devil's Ride," Diego said into my ear, over the sound of the music. "I won it on his TV show contest. She has an S&S Twin V engine and Baker six-speed transmission."

"Impressive. I'd like to see that bathroom now."

He laughed. "She has zero miles on the clock. One day, I might take you out on her."

"I'd like that."

"If I ever do, you'll know you're special. She's worth eighty thousand dollars."

"Cheap," I joked.

He led me to the bathroom. No. This couldn't happen again.

"Colby?" He said. There was a question in his eyes.

I answered it by backing up against the wall.

Diego locked the door and flicked off the light. The subdued, velvety atmosphere only added to my mounting arousal.

"Let me take you to the moon." He bit my earlobe, and not gently, either. He was breathing hard.

The flash of pain morphed into desire and my cock hardened. Fuck, I wanted him bad. Instead, I tried to push him back.

He ignored me and scooted down to his knees and undid my jeans, liberating my cock. Somewhere, a tap dripped, and I stared up at his artificial moonlight as he began to suck me, slowly and with total assuredness. I had to find the strength to stay away from him.

I began to struggle. "Diego no. Damn it."

His cell phone rang, and it saved me this time.

He pulled back and checked the readout. I saw the frown on his face. He looked pale in the moonlight. I wasn't sure what was bothering him more, the call or me telling him "no."

"What the fuck happened?" he rasped.

I struggled with my zipper.

"Get dressed," he whispered to me. "We got problems."

"What problems?" I whispered back as he turned on the lights again.

"Somebody just burned up your sister's bakery," he said, his expression tense.

"Holy shit! Are they okay?"

"Bring 'em back here," Diego said into the phone. He looked at me. "Your family's fine. My guys are bringin' 'em here."

I followed him outside. "The TCs are claiming responsibility. Franklin Kennedy's the one who threw the first Molotov cocktail into the joint, knowing your sister's kids were in there. I'm gonna fuck up this prick, big time."

"That's my job," I said as I got on the back of his bike.

"Mine," he roared. "He killed one of my men. Jax went in to get the kids and caught fire."

We sped back to the bike shop. His crew milled around, everyone talking at once. I was surprised to see my father, a doubled-over Jerry, and Calvin, all in there.

"You gotta pledge allegiance now," Diego said. "No time for fancy stuff. That'll have to wait." He looked at each of us in turn. I heard the sound of spitting and turned to find Nuts in the doorway, working on a new bag of sunflower seeds.

I couldn't comprehend the TCs going after my family this way. Jerry and I had never done business like that. Never had, never would. I pledged allegiance, my brain and teeth chattering. I could have lost my sister.

"Let's go," Diego said to me.

I fixed my gaze on him. Thank God he was taking me with him. We walked into the room with his Britten bike.

"We're taking that?" I was shocked.

"Yeah. We're about to get apocalyptic on his ass."

He unlocked the glass case, my father and Marcel appearing out of nowhere to help us move the bike to the shop floor.

I realized two things as Diego got on that incredible machine. I realized everything he said about the sound and speed was right.

As we practically flew out of the room and out the back door, I smelled burning rubber, and my heart thundered in my chest as I realized the second thing.

I could easily fall in love with Diego if I didn't watch my step. *Fucking, fucking hell.* I held on tight. It was as though we'd always ridden this way. I stared up at the sky. Suddenly, for the first time ever, I wasn't alone.

I realized another thing.

I liked it.

You may also enjoy the following from eXtasy Books Inc:

Moonlight Seduction
A.J. Llewellyn and D.J. Manly

Excerpt

Colby turned to me, his head on the pillow beside me. "Can you take Kennedy?"

"Yes."

"You mean it?"

"I mean it."

"I've never seen an extreme fight. I know someone dies at the end. Are there weapons?"

"No guns, but apart from that, there are no rules."

He turned away. "Jesus Christ."

I didn't know what to say. "Why this sudden concern for my welfare?" I guess I wanted to hear the words. He didn't have to say he loved me. He probably didn't. "Colby. It's okay to care, doesn't mean we're . . . you know. No strings."

"Fuck you, Diego," he said. He started to get out of bed.

I put a hand on his arm. "Wait. You're angry at me."

He turned around and for a moment didn't say anything. He just looked at me. Then he sprang on me, lying on me. He pinned my arms to the mattress and captured my mouth.

He kissed me passionately, then moved down the length of me, licking me and suckling me. He stroked and sucked my cock and my balls, and I was erect again.

"Damn you, Colby," I muttered. I made a grab for him, and we rolled off the bed onto the floor. I took him there on all fours, holding him prisoner in my arms while he pretended to struggle. But we both knew what he wanted. I tightened my hold and fucked him hard while he cried out. Finally, Colby said my name while I rubbed his cock and his nipples and rode him even harder on the carpet.

We came on our knees, his back against my chest and I held him in my arms until his breathing returned to normal. He rubbed his head under my chin, then turned and held me, his lips touching my shoulder. He kissed my ear and then whispered, "I hate you for this."

I released him. His words shocked the hell out of me. I stared at him, speechless.

He reached up to touch my face, but I pushed his hand away. "Don't."

"You don't understand," he said. His eyes were bright with tears. "If I love you, I'll lose you. I lost my mother and my sister. I loved them too much. Kennedy will take you from me, and that will be it." He got up and looked down at me. He took my chin and lifted my face. "But if I don't love you, you'll be okay. I can have you when I want."

I shook my head and stood up. "No. You can't, Colby," I said. "When your membership in this club is final, it will be the end of us like this. We have to stop." It broke my heart, but it had to be said. "I can't be your lover."

ABOUT THE AUTHORS

A.J. Llewellyn is the author of almost three hundred published gay romance novels. A.J. lives in California, but dreams of living in Hawaii. Frequent trips to all the islands, bags of Kona coffee in the fridge and a healthy collection of Hawaiian records keep A.J. refueled.

A.J's passion for the islands led to writing a play about the last ruling monarch of Hawaii, Queen Lili'uokalani. A.J. has written a non-erotic novel about the overthrow of her kingdom written in diary form from her maid's point of view.

A.J. never lacks inspiration for male/male erotic romances and has to prise fingers from the computer keyboard to pursue other passions: collecting books on Hawaiiana, surfing and spending time with family, friends and animal companions.

D.J. Manly: I write not only for my own pleasure but for the pleasure of my readers. I can't remember a time in my life when I haven't written and told stories. When I'm not writing, I'm dreaming about writing, doing something wild and adventurous, or trying to make the world a better and more open-minded place to live in. I adore beautiful men, and I know I'm not alone in this! Eroticism between consenting adults, in all its many forms, is the icing on the cake of life!

D.J. has published well over two hundred novels/novellas and is a well-seasoned writer.

www.ingramcontent.com/pod-product-compliance
Lightning Source LLC
Chambersburg PA
CBHW071625140626

46555CB00021B/457